PENGUIN BOOKS

A GLIMPSE OF SION'S GLORY

Isabel Colegate's other novels are *The Blackmailer* (1958), *A Man of Power* (1960) and *The Great Occasion* (1962), published by Penguin in one volume in 1984; *Statues in a Garden* (1964; Penguin 1983); the Orlando trilogy, comprising *Orlando King* (1968), *Orlando at the Brazen Threshold* (1971) and *Agatha* (1973), published by Penguin in one volume in 1984; *News from the City of the Sun* (1979); and *The Shooting Party* (1980), for which she received the W. H. Smith Annual Literary Award for 1981.

Isabel Colegate is married with three children and lives near Bath.

By the same author

The Blackmailer
A Man of Power
The Great Occasion
Statues in a Garden
Orlando King
Orlando at the Brazen Threshold
Agatha
News from the City of the Sun
The Shooting Party

ISABEL COLEGATE

A Glimpse of
Sion's Glory

PENGUIN BOOKS

Penguin Books Ltd, Harmondsworth, Middlesex, England
Viking Penguin Inc., 40 West 23rd Street, New York, New York 10010, U.S.A.
Penguin Books Australia Ltd, Ringwood, Victoria, Australia
Penguin Books Canada Limited, 2801 John Street, Markham, Ontario, Canada L3R 1B4
Penguin Books (N.Z.) Ltd, 182–190 Wairau Road, Auckland 10, New Zealand

First published in the USA by Viking/Elisabeth Sifton Books 1985
First published in Great Britain by Hamish Hamilton 1985
Published in Penguin Books 1986

Printed and bound in Great Britain by
Cox & Wyman Ltd, Reading

Contents

The Girl Who Had Lived Among Artists

She had lived among artists; her way of looking at things was different. At least, that was what he told himself.

He was a village boy, though his mother would have it he was something better. She, the mother, came from a social level at which it was enormously important to know that there was a lower one; there were undoubtedly several higher; she claimed that marriage had exalted her to one of these. Her husband, the father of the boy, had been a vet; he died before the boy was born. Somewhere in the vet's not too remote ancestry had been a lord; it was this to which the widow clung. She felt it gave her, in the village in which they lived in something approaching penury (for this was all before the age of supplementary benefits), a natural right to a certain sort of relationship with the Vicar's wife, and a certain sort of distant look at her lowlier neighbours when collecting her children from the village school.

The boy, whose name was Vere ('A family name on my husband's side'), had an elder sister, Marjorie, who explained to him one day that his mother was a snob, because she had been rude to the mother of Marjorie's best friend Joan. Joan's father was the blacksmith and her mother, who had dark hair and a face which looked as if it had somehow missed the last stage of its manufacture, leaving the features not quite defined, had come of a family of tinkers who had camped on the village green the summer after the War (the First War that was).

'She thinks Joan's not good enough for us because our great uncle was a lord. She thinks we ought never to speak

3

to anyone but the Vicar and Mrs Hardy and the people from the Hall. She's always sucking up to Mrs Hardy, going up to the Vicarage wearing gloves and taking that horrid seed cake.'

'Seed cake, ugh!' said Vere.

He concealed his surprise at his sister's remarks because when he revealed ignorance she told him he was stupid. He had failed to notice his mother's attitude to Joan's mother, just as he had thought she went to see Mrs Hardy because she liked her and wore gloves because her hands were cold. He was eleven and Marjorie was thirteen. Marjorie despised her mother. Her mother told the Vicar's wife that Marjorie was going through a phase.

'Is our great uncle really a lord?' asked Vere.

'Shouldn't think so. We wouldn't be eating boiled fish all day if he was. Joan has mutton chops for tea.'

'Every day?' asked Vere, very much impressed.

'Most days probably,' said Marjorie airily, having no idea.

This disclosure pushed the news about the great uncle temporarily out of Vere's mind, but when he thought about it later on he rather liked the idea; only he wished his mother would not speak of it, because she spoilt it. He built no expectations upon the relationship himself, he thought of it consciously quite seldom, but just at the back of his mind was the thought that probably somewhere in his blood there was something remotely glorious. Possibly it was simply that most of the time he felt so extraordinarily well.

The fish van came to the village every Tuesday and Friday, and parked on the green for an hour or two in the morning. Mrs Turner, Vere's mother, was a regular client. Boiled cod was more economical than meat and every now and then could be enlivened by a parsley sauce, in this case usually on the lumpy side. The vet had been a poor financial manager, a lazy easy-going man who sometimes failed to collect his debts and sometimes lost an unexpectedly large

4

sum on a locally fancied runner in the races at Bath or Wincanton. He left his widow virtually penniless. All the rest of their lives the smell of boiled fish brought back both to Marjorie and to Vere a number of different feelings, none of them particularly pleasant. Guilt was among the feelings, and a kind of hopeless regret. They had had in many ways a happy childhood, but after quite an early age neither of them had much cared for their mother. She spent too much time nagging them on class grounds. Their manners were not good enough for children of such ancestry, they used the wrong phrases, had the wrong friends, didn't care what they looked like. The later realization that all this had been an attempt to arm them for a struggle they never then gave a thought to, a struggle for existence in a harsh world in which they had nothing much in the way of weapons and in which their simple manners and country accents could only count against them, made them guilty though not in retrospect more tolerant. She was an embarrassing mother. She played too much on the idea, believing it implicitly herself (this was England, between the wars), that a connexion however tenuous with the upper class gave her a right to a different kind of social consideration from that appropriate to the great majority of her neighbours. She thought herself a cut above them.

She had probably less money and certainly less practical ability. She was an incompetent housekeeper; it was this as much as the nagging which irritated her children. They failed to understand that it was a congenital weakness and not one which could be blamed upon her snobbery. She was incompetent not because she thought herself too fine a lady to concern herself with household matters, but because of a basic incapacity which no amount of trying (for she did try) seemed to be able to overcome. The three of them lived in a muddle of boiled fish and unwashed dishes, second-hand clothes, unpaid bills, borrowed finery for a village wedding, borrowed garden tools to mow the little strip of lawn and cultivate the vegetable patch. She was shameless in her sponging, perhaps because she looked on it as being all for the sake of the children. So relentless was she in pursuit of that which she wished to borrow that even when once she went up to the Vicarage to ask whether she might borrow a pickling saucepan – a request which Mrs Hardy, a person of quite average kindliness, would have granted without a moment's thought to anyone else – and heard Mrs Hardy, meeting her husband in the hall on her way to fetch the desired object from the kitchen, say to him, 'Mrs Ask-and-it-shall-be-Given-unto-You is here again,' even then she chose to think of the remark as affectionate, and as showing what old friends she and the Hardys had become. After all, didn't she always return what she borrowed? Nearly always, anyway.

The Hardys were held up to the children as models. The Farquhars, who lived at the Hall, were remote, and despite Mrs Turner's efforts remained so. They would have been better suited to her purposes, for they were gentry; the Vicar and Mrs Hardy were not. The blood in their veins came on both sides from generations of evangelical Christians but it was not blue. Mrs Turner vaguely sensed this but all her class lore had been learned from her husband the vet, and since he had not been there to consult for some years now her expertise was not all it might have been. She taught the children to carry clean handkerchieves and when they sneezed to say, 'Beg pardon'. She told them it was common to say 'Lavvy' and that they must say 'Round the corner' instead. She told them never to wear their shirt collars outside their jackets and encouraged them to follow Mrs Hardy's example and raise their little fingers slightly when lifting a teacup to their lips. They paid very little attention. The veneer of gentility she would have liked to have applied to their rusticity did not stick.

Those were snobbish times. The snobbery of England in the 1930s was the real thing. In the *Bath Chronicle* in those days ladies advertising for domestic servants would add 'Radstock girls need not apply'. Radstock girls were of coal-mining stock, the lowest of the low. Vere's friend Carley the lorry-driver, who died for love of Nancy, the girl who had lived among artists, came from Radstock. His four brothers followed his father down the pit; only Carley diverged. All four brothers and both parents came to the funeral, though Carley had told Vere he had seen none of them for years. They were small people, whose pinched white faces bore on that occasion identical looks of puzzled shame. Anyone who had known Carley might have been forgiven for wondering whether the bent old mother in her unimaginable youth could have played the father false; for no one could deny that Carley was a handsome man.

*

When Vere left school he went to work in a small car repair workshop on the south side of the river in Bath. Mrs Turner persuaded the Vicar to let him have his old bicycle; she said the job depended on it. The bicycle was very old, and in due course the Vicar bought a new one, so Mrs Turner was easily able to persuade herself she had done him a favour. After a year of struggling up and down the five miles of hilly road between the garage and the village, Vere had sufficiently made his mark with Mr Bodman his employer for the latter to finance the purchase of a less ancient machine, a well-maintained second-hand Raleigh with three gears.

The new bicycle became Vere's passion. He sped up and down the Somerset hills, matching himself against cars on the open road or rhythmically conquering the crests and launching himself with a vigorous thrust upon the downward slopes, attaining now and then such total absorption in physical movement as to be in a kind of ecstasy. Furnished with a book from the Bath Public Library on Bicycle Maintenance from A to Z, he became intimately acquainted

7

with every bolt and screw of his machine, could renew the gears, change the brake rubbers, align the wheels, replace their spokes. The mending of punctures became a matter of minutes. In the course of time clients materialized; among the bicyclists of that part of Bath known as Holloway his skill attained for him a modest fame.

Holloway was the old beggars' quarter. In the eighteenth century, when Bath was a smart resort, the visiting grandees who had come to take the waters would sometimes have themselves driven across the river from the fashionable part of the town and pass up and down the narrow streets to stare at the poor; to shudder, or sigh, or laugh, or toss a coin, or shake their heads at the sorry spectacle of moral degeneracy. Holloway was still a poor quarter in the 1930s; after the war the planners pulled down the terraces of pleasant little eighteenth-century houses, presumably because of their association with the bad old days.

Bodman Car Bodies was at the bottom of the hill, by the river. Its yard was full of old cars, waiting to be plundered for parts needed for slightly more roadworthy vehicles. A corner of the long dark workshop became Vere's; the bicycle repair side of Bodman's Car Bodies flourished. He fixed up a system of pulleys, by which machines in need of more than mere puncture mending could be hoisted up into a convenient position for the repairer. He was proud of this corner which was entirely his own; he never left it at night without a last look at the neat array of tools and the suspended bicycles. He would go back sometimes and adjust the angle of one of these, on purely visual grounds.

It was on an evening when he was lingering in this way that Carley wandered in, and stood watching him as he very slightly lowered one of the bicycles which was on the pulley, stood back to look at it, re-adjusted it, stood back again and nodded.

'What are you trying to do then?' asked Carley, puzzled.

Vere, startled, turned to see in the shadowy light of the workshop (the spring evening through the open doors behind him) himself when thirty – or so he obscurely recognized. It was simply that they were the same physical type, fairish, thick-set, strong and well-balanced – the sort of physique you sometimes see in cricketers – but the boy, being only seventeen, was slighter.

'Adjusting,' he mumbled, unable to explain.

The man nodded.

'Give us a hand will you?' Mr Bodman looked round the door. 'Bolts are stuck.'

They both went out into the late spring evening light in the yard, and looked at the lorry's punctured tyre. First one and then the other tried to loosen the bolts so as to remove the wheel. They were rusty and dry. With several hammer blows on a heavy spanner Vere loosened one. Carley took the hammer and loosened the others. They smiled at each other, acknowledging physical strength, an attribute they shared.

After that Carley came to the workshop quite often. He worked as a driver for a small firm of carriers, whose vehicles were often in need of maintenance. He had a big Alsatian bitch which followed him everywhere. He was mildly amused by Vere's bicycling expertise, of which he approved in a lazy way (for Carley despite his fine physique never seemed to take any exercise at all). Conversation about the dog, the bicycles, the lorry, Carley's latest long-distance journey, the weather, led to the kind of friendly but not intimate relationship which Vere had developed with several of Mr Bodman's regular customers. It was the dog which turned the thing into a friendship. She had puppies; towards the end of the pregnancy and during the two months before the puppies could leave her she could no longer go with Carley on all his journeys. He asked Vere to look after her.

'She seems to like you. You could stay at my place while I'm away – there's a room. It's small but – just while I'm away.'

It was more of a cupboard really, in the basement flat of the house in Henrietta Street. It was a fine Georgian terrace house in the more genteel part of Bath but there was damp in the basement, more particularly in the little back pantry under the stairs where Vere slept. There was a window though, opening onto the back yard where the puppies lived. Vere was happy there and when the puppies grew older and were sold for five shillings each – except for one, Rosie, the friendliest bitch – Vere asked if he could pay rent and stay on for a bit. '. . . for the winter,' he said. 'I get a bit sick of bicycling home in the dark.'

His mother was not pleased. It meant she would be alone because Marjorie had gone into service and taken a job in London (she'd served her first few years locally and had such a good reference that the London job was a step up, second housemaid to a household where they kept three). Vere promised to go home at weekends and to see to all the jobs around the house she needed – mending things, chopping wood – and all the time he lived in Bath he did so, even at the height of the crisis, when sometimes he could only spare a Sunday afternoon. Windless autumn afternoons splitting logs furiously, as if it could atone.

*

The house in Henrietta Street belonged to Mrs Wilson Clark. There used to be a cook and butler living in the basement flat but after the Major's death Mrs Wilson Clark found her widow's pension inadequate, and though she was occasionally lucky on the Stock Exchange thought it prudent to let the basement and manage with a Cook General who lived on the top floor. When times got harder still the Cook General moved down to the second floor into the little room next to Mrs Wilson Clark's daughter Elaine's room; the top floor was made into a self-contained flat and let to Professor and Mrs Behr, who had recently arrived from Vienna.

Mrs Wilson Clark did not care for Carley whom she thought a very low sort of man, but owing to the damp and the fact that she had no intention of paying for the place to be redecorated her choice of tenants was not large. Carley was not particular. He scrubbed the place out thoroughly his first weekend – it smelled of tobacco and he was not a smoker – he had few possessions and those he had he kept very neatly. There was the dogs' box, an old gramophone and some jazz records. He gave Vere permission to play the gramophone when he was not there. He was quite often out, sometimes at the pub, sometimes Vere understood with women, but they were never brought to the flat. Vere was shy with him because he did not speak much; also Vere, having lived all his life with only his mother and sister, found a masculine presence slightly alarming; he treated Carley with respect. During the first few months the only time they lost their reserve was when they were playing with the dogs. Bess was a fine specimen of her breed; Rosie already took after her. Even one of them would have been too large for such a small flat; two were certainly excessive. On the other hand Carley had trained Bess to absolute obedience and soon had Rosie on the same path. Vere was more indulgent; he preferred to play. This was a noisy business, tending towards destruction of the furniture. Rosie in particular kept up a continuous deep growling interrupted by puppyish yelps of excitement, a comical sound which Vere loved to evoke. He would roll about the sitting-room floor in a prolonged scuffle with Rosie into which Bess usually threw herself with an enthusiasm not compatible with maternal dignity; Carley would some-times join in.

It was on one such occasion that Mrs Wilson Clark, returning from a charity tea party, looked down into her basement window and though vague in her suspicions as to exactly what kind of frightfulness was taking place, was sufficiently alarmed to hurry into the house and telephone the police.

What had happened was that Carley had come in wearing his flat cap, and had taken it off and thrown it across the room (the front door of the flat opened straight into the sitting-room) towards a coat stand which stood in the corner at rather an odd angle because one of the three legs had come half-adrift from the central column and gave the whole thing a list to one side. The dogs, who had hurried up to give him their usual welcome, took this to be an invitation to a game, and Rosie in her eagerness being quicker than her mother leapt into the air and caught the cap before it reached the stand. Bess fell upon her, Carley shouted at them both, Vere coming in from the kitchen pulled the cap away from Rosie and threw it to Carley. Carley caught it and threw it back over the heads of the leaping dogs, Vere trying to catch it fell upon the sofa, Rosie jumped on top of him, Vere threw the cap to Carley, who jumping to catch it fell over the armchair and was joyfully attacked by both dogs, who were in turn fallen upon by Vere, who was shouting to Carley, 'Give it here, give it here,' above the growling and yelping of the dogs. Mrs Wilson Clark told the police that there were several men fighting on the floor and any number of dogs trying to kill them.

*

Mrs Wilson Clark was of rather remarkable physical appearance, a fact put down by her Bath acquaintance to her mother's having been American. She wore an orange wig and a good deal of rouge. She had spent much of her married life in India, to which the Major had taken her as a young bride from Tunbridge Wells (for the American mother was quite Anglicized and respectably married to a Kentish optician). India had ruined her complexion, deprived her of most of her hair (after a bad bout of malaria), and bored her. The fact was that 'the Major' had not been in the Army at all; his widow had given him military rank after his death. In life he had been a businessman, a box-wallah; and among box-wallahs the least exalted, a jute-wallah, and among the jute-wallahs not exalted at all, a clerk in a huge warehouse in Bombay, working for a firm of indeed the highest respectability, but working in a humble capacity. The Wilson Clarks belonged to a Club, at which they spent a good deal of time, having tea or drinks, playing tennis or bridge, but the Club, though of course no Indian could have belonged to it, was definitely inferior, socially speaking, to at least three other Clubs in Bombay. The circle in which the Wilson Clarks moved was a severely restricted one, and Mona Wilson Clark was a livelier character than most. One evening after a *thé dansant* with alcoholic refreshments she took a tumble from the verandah into the Club's most flamboyant flower bed and found her circle even more restricted. After the Major's sudden death from a fever (he'd never been a robust man) the widower and the pale child Elaine left India with relief. The Tunbridge Wells optician having died and left her a surprisingly comfortable sum and a good deal of heavy Victorian silver, she retired to Bath, acquired a wig, promoted her late husband to a military majority, and soon assumed quite a prominent position in Bath society.

'It is not at all proper,' she said. 'Not at all what I had in mind when I advertised for a quiet single tenant. The Mayor was present at the tea, you know.'

Carley nodded, and said encouragingly 'Oh yes?'

He recognized that having tea with the Mayor meant a great deal to Mrs Wilson Clark. It was not his idea of fun but he was quite prepared to allow that it might be hers. He was generous about that sort of thing.

'Rough-housing,' she said loftily. 'Horse-play. Noisy horse-play.'

'It was the dogs . . .' Vere said, smiling to invite complicity in deploring the silly creatures.

Mrs Wilson Clark suspected insolence.

'I know they were dogs,' she said.

Vere smiled even more ingratiatingly, to reassure her that he had not meant to imply that she had mistaken them for horses. 'One's a pup, you see.'

'Have I given permission for dogs to be kept in my basement?'

'Ah,' said Carley, who had not thought of this. 'No, I can't say you have given permission, ma'am, not specifically . . .'

Mrs Wilson Clark was silent for a few moments. She was a bit of a bully. If they had seemed afraid of her she would probably have turned them out of the flat there and then; but they hardly even looked shamefaced. She liked boldness, though she would never have admitted it. The police constable whom she had called (and whose bicycle was regularly repaired by Vere) had spoken well of their characters; she decided to raise their rent rather than evict them. When they had convinced her that their earnings were inadequate to meet her demands, a compromise was reached. They would pay an extra two shillings a week and Vere, when he came home from work in the evenings, would carry the coal from the coal hole under the pavement not only to Mrs Wilson Clark's first floor drawing-room but all the way upstairs to Professor and Mrs Behr's top floor flat. Thus Betsy the maid was relieved of a duty which had been causing her to threaten to give notice, and Vere became a familiar figure up and down the stairs in the house in Henrietta Street. 'The coal boy' Mrs Wilson Clark called him to her friends as they sat playing bridge by the fire. 'Put the decanter on the sherry tray,' she would tell him sometimes, and he would fetch the heavy cut-glass decanter from the cupboard and place it with some solemnity on the Benares bronze tray she'd brought

14

from India; Mrs Wilson Clark's friends were favourably impressed.

★

One morning when Carley had been away on a long journey to the North, Vere came back from taking the dogs for their early morning run in Henrietta Gardens and found Nancy sitting on the sofa, wrapped in a Paisley shawl.

It was half past seven on the 17th of April 1938. There had been sunlight in the gardens and the dogs had run, exercising each other, while he had sat on a bench, eating the piece of bread and margarine he had brought with him for his breakfast and looking across the intervening trees up to the curve of Camden Crescent on the hill opposite; there were no other buildings to be seen from there, only the short stubby spire of the Church of St John the Baptist, Mrs Wilson Clark's place of worship. He had called the dogs and walked home. There was no need to put them on their leads for there were no roads to cross. They had only to walk along a few yards of pavement, past the houses at the end of the terrace, and down the stone steps to the basement, where the light was on, though he was sure he had left it off, and where there was Nancy, wrapped in a Paisley shawl. He had never seen anything so surprising.

'She was stranded,' said Carley, 'in Edinburgh.'

He came out of the kitchen, holding two mugs of tea.

'I've just made some if you want it,' he gestured with his head backwards towards the kitchen.

'No thanks, I've had some. I've got to go.'

'Her name's Nancy. Nancy – Vere.'

She took the tea and put it on the table beside her. Then she threw back the shawl and stretched herself. She wore a skimpy black dress, black stockings and no shoes.

'He saved my life,' she said, smiling at Carley.

Carley went back into the kitchen. Vere stood looking at

15

Nancy. Nancy continued to smile. It was a thing she never minded, being stared at.

He did not think her beautiful, merely utterly extra-ordinary.

★

She scattered Paisley shawls all over the place; it seemed they were all she had. She spread them over the lumpy sofa and the armchair whose springs had gone, and the big bed she shared with Carley.

Vere, whose coal-carrying had made him the general messenger and means of communication within the house-hold in Henrietta Street, in due course found himself having to explain Nancy. He always had time to stop and talk. In those days, what's more, he liked everybody. He liked Mrs Wilson Clark, her orange wig, her scarlet cheeks, the elaborate show of gentility which usually quite failed to conceal a vulgarity beneath which he recognized a childish longing for a good time. He even quite liked her bridge friends, with their incessant smoking and their frequent recourse to the decanter on the Benares bronze tray. Not that he thought of them much, but when he did he thought of them as nice people. Mrs Wilson Clark's daughter Elaine was nice too, no one could deny that. She was unfailingly kind, good, helpful and nervously in need of reassurance. She meekly gave in to her mother on every point and crept off every now and then in her hat and gloves to the meeting of the Literary Society or a concert at the Pump Room. She never dreamt of leaving her mother – for who would do the weekly grocery order or arrange the flowers? – and put her fairly continuous unhappiness down to her headaches, rather than the other way round. She had become fond of Vere and had lent him one or two books published by the Society for the Propagation of Christian Knowledge.

Professor Behr took an interest in Vere too; his cause was not Christianity so much as Europe.

16

'Europe is one,' he told Vere. 'The European consciousness is one consciousness. The European soul is one soul.
Frontiers should be abolished. This I am working for. The
youth of Europe should come together with cultural
joyousness. Young men like you should be the brothers in
art of my cousins Heinrich and Ferdinand, my charming
niece Maria, my godson Franz who is, I am sorry to say, a
little fat. This we are trying through the International PEN
Club to encourage. You know International PEN?'

'Not exactly, no,' said Vere, adding kindly if not quite
truthfully, 'I've heard of it though.'

'PEN. We are the writers of the world. In my own
country . . .' but he stopped, as if suddenly disheartened,
and took off his pince-nez to wipe them slowly with a silk
handkerchief.

'In his own country,' said his wife Hilda, 'he is very
well-known.'

Hilda Behr reminded Vere of Miss Rawson at the village
school whose deeply hostile gaze could hypnotize you into
wiping your nose on the back of your hand, thus becoming
worthy of the scorn her eyes already expressed.

'You have heard of Thomas Mann? Heinrich Mann,
Werfel, Freud, Einstein? Fritz Behr is of their number. He
walks with them upon the intellectual mountain tops.'

Vere might have said that he knew someone – Mr
Bodman's nephew in fact – who had recently spent his
Easter holidays climbing in the Brecon Beacons; but instinct told him that would be a mistake, and he obeyed his
instinct, though without knowing why it was right.

'I expect you'll be wanting to get back there then before
long,' he said instead to Mr Behr who was looking small
and unhappy as he usually did when his wife spoke. 'To
your own country I mean.'

'All is not well there,' said Fritz Behr sadly. 'All is not
well. But in England you are only interested in sport. Not in
serious discussion.'

'Miss Elaine is very serious. And I've not heard her mention sport at all.'

Later on Elaine told him that she had taken Professor and Mrs Behr to a concert in the recently re-opened Assembly Rooms and that she thought they had enjoyed it, but though she and Mrs Behr remained on friendly terms, the Professor was more elusive and tended to put on his sad look when Elaine spoke to him.

'You don't come up to his Viennese standards, dear,' said Mrs Wilson Clark. 'Not plump enough. I know these Continentals.'

Certainly he seemed to prefer the mother to the daughter. The assortment of often repeated prejudices which served her instead of thought hardly came up to his ideal of serious discussion, but there was a kind of conviviality about her, and he was lonely.

'Where is comradeship in this cold country?' he would say to his cold wife Hilda (she had been his secretary and he had married her so as to have someone to look after him in his exile). 'Where is art or philosophy or joy?'

'Why ask me? It was you who brought me here. The home of everything most calm and refined in English culture, you said. The beautiful Palladian city. It is a shell. No life, no art, no culture. Nothing but respectability.'

'I am so sorry, my dear, it is all my fault,' he would answer humbly.

But when Nancy's presence became known throughout the household it was Hilda Behr who was most emphatic in her denunciation of the newcomer on the grounds of her lack of just that respectability of which she had so recently been complaining.

'She is not a respectable woman. To pretend anything else is English hypocrisy.'

It was not until Nancy had been living in the flat for several weeks that her presence was noticed. Comings and goings from the basement were seldom observed from

above and it was only when Mrs Wilson Clark had happened to be approaching or leaving her own front door on
several different occasions when Nancy had been apparent
on the basement's steps that the landlady gave voice to her
curiosity. It had been aroused of course the very first time
she had seen Nancy. On that occasion Nancy had been
going down the stone steps with the Paisley shawl wrapt
loosely round her bent head and over her shoulders, her
smooth face with its high cheek-bones showing white
through the spring dusk, her aspect mysterious, melancholy, poetic. Mrs Wilson Clark had put her down as Vere's
sister, since she knew he had one; but she felt the attribution
not quite satisfactory and perhaps only made it to prevent
her imagination running riot. She knew she had a tendency
to dramatize, and felt it right to try to resist it. 'Now,
Elaine, it's no use fancying things,' she would say. But
Elaine, though she did fancy things sometimes, kept her
fancies to herself and never let them interfere with her
behaviour (though she suspected they were not terribly
good for her headaches).

The next time Mrs Wilson Clark saw Nancy she was not
wearing the shawl. She was running up the steps with the
two dogs and laughing. When she saw Mrs Wilson Clark
she said 'Hallo' and went on laughing. Then she called the
dogs and ran towards the Park. Mrs Wilson Clark recognized that something remarkable had happened in Henrietta
Street though she was not yet certain what it was. It might
have been an effect of the light.

'You must introduce me to your sister,' she said graciously to Vere when next he came in to fetch her coal scuttle for
refilling.

'I'd like to,' said Vere. 'But she's down at London most of
the time.'

'Is she not staying with you now? I thought I'd seen her.'

'Oh no, that's not Marjorie. That's Nancy.'

'Nancy?'

'A friend of Carley's.' Here memories of Mrs Wilson Clark's attitude when she heard of the presence of the dogs intervened, and Vere became cautious. 'A very old friend. Just stopping for a visit.'

'Oh really? Where is her home?'

'Edinburgh. That's why she stays a while when she comes here, being such a long way.'

'I know it well. Delightful town. A little like Bath in some ways, but grey you know where Bath is golden. The Queen City of the West, I always call it, Bath I mean. Edinburgh of course is the Athens of the North but that's on account of the University, naturally.'

'Naturally,' said Vere, who no longer found any difficulty in conversation with Mrs Wilson Clark; he treated it as a kind of plainsong.

In due course the revelation on the steps was vouchsafed to Professor Behr. He followed after it keenly, offered it his arm, entered into animated conversation, pronounced it a perfectly delightful young lady. It was at this stage that Mrs Behr began to speak of respectability.

The Behrs were occasionally asked by Mrs Wilson Clark to take a hand of bridge with Elaine and herself after supper on a quiet evening when she had no other engagements (it was not to be expected that the Behrs or Elaine would have engagements). It was not a specially happy thought. Mrs Wilson Clark was partnered by Elaine, Hilda by her husband. When Elaine once suggested that they might cut for partners, the suggestion was not followed up and she was told afterwards by her mother that the Professor must have thought her very forward; so they played in family pairs. Mrs Wilson Clark bullied Elaine and Hilda bullied the Professor. The Professor was by far the best, as well as the most patient, player. Elaine was dreadfully hesitant, though as she never seemed to have any card higher than a ten her opportunities for choice were few.

On one such evening they discussed Nancy, her continued presence having by now impinged upon the consciousness of all of them; Hilda made known her feelings as to respectability. The evening ended with Mrs Wilson Clark declaring her intention of going down to the basement flat first thing tomorrow morning and turning her out.

*

It seemed that Nancy had a grandmother living in Tunbridge Wells, the widow of a dentist – a very well-to-do dentist, Mrs Wilson Clark said, for she remembered the family, and their big white house somewhere on the slopes of Mount Ephraim and the bridge evenings to which Mrs Wilson Clark's mother, the American wife of the Tunbridge Wells optician, used to go all those years ago before the Great War – 'Isn't it a co-incidence?' – and the son whom Mrs Wilson Clark just faintly remembered at tennis parties – 'but I was too young, not grown-up, they all seemed so handsome' – had been, it transpired, a hero – '*so* brave', Nancy said, 'and *so* many medals and he was killed at somewhere called Loos and my mother threw everything out of the window, but everything, chairs, tables, books, plates, anything she could lift; and because she was angry I thought it was all my fault. I thought he'd left us and it was my fault because I'd told her about the other woman. I'd seen her, when he was on leave just before, I'd seen him walking along the street with her when I was on the way back from the Park with the girl who looked after me. We were living in London in a flat. He stopped and lifted me up and introduced me to her and said, don't you think she's pretty? I suppose he thought I was too young to remember. I'm sure he didn't ask me not to say I'd seen them and of course I did, as soon as he came in. I was in the sitting-room with my mother – it was after tea – and he came in and I said, where's the pretty lady you were with? And there was the most frightful scene and I was hustled out of the room and I

21

heard them shouting at each other and then of course he had
to go and then the telegram came so I thought it was to say
he'd gone off with the pretty lady.'

And then there had been the years of poverty because it
transpired that he had lost his money gambling with his
Army friends and had left them nothing, and her mother
took in dressmaking and the two of them got terribly on
each other's nerves until the Artist appeared, with some
sewing to be done for some amateur theatricals (what
amateur theatricals? She could not remember; amateur
theatricals in St John's Wood) and had taken her away and
prevented her, she said, from dying of boredom. She had
been fifteen.

The Artist had taught her how to cook. He had taught her
a number of other things, but it was the cooking which was
the first of Nancy's revelations really to impinge upon Vere.
Her looks, and her eye for the looks of everything else,
might be supposed to have come first, but in fact the
concepts they involved were so unfamiliar and so new that
their impact took some time to sink in. Well-prepared food,
though equally unfamiliar, was immediately appreciable. It
was not until after at least a week that Vere understood that
what was different about Nancy's looks was that she was
beautiful; once he grasped this fact its impression upon him
was enormous. He never ceased to wonder at it, nor did
anything that subsequently occurred alter his faith in her
supremacy in this respect. As for the way in which a few
Paisley shawls, a little re-arrangement of the furniture,
some scrubbing, some fiddling about with lamps, changed
completely the whole atmosphere and aspect of the basement flat, that too took some time to make its effect. When
it did, it slightly but quite irrevocably changed the world. It
was as if even the landscape he had loved before he had
loved for its parts and not for its whole. He had never seen it
whole; just as he had never seen the house he lived in from
the outside, or the flagstones of the pavement wet in the

rain, or the way the dusk lowered a faint veil of violet over Victoria Park and made the view up over the trees to Camden Crescent mysteriously less reasonable than in the morning light. It was as if an invisible membrane had been removed from his eyes or a part of his brain alerted which had slept until then; all the rest of his life he saw in a different way from the way in which he had seen before.

The Artist had lived in Paris, in the Artists' Quarter, before the Great War. He had been poor, living only on such pictures as he could sell, and he had had a French mistress who had taught him what wonders could be done with a few bones and two or three leeks, or a cabbage and a piece of bacon. This knowledge, which had been passed on in the smallest detail to Nancy, was combined in her case with a wonderful neatness and efficiency in the performance of all household tasks. She possessed in the highest degree the capacity to make her hearth, temporary though it might turn out to be, a place of respite and calm. There were, however, intermissions.

One morning she did not get out of bed. She was not ill, she said. When Carley and Vere came back in the evening the flat was as they had left it and she was still in bed. She repeated that she was not ill, that she didn't want anything, that they should go away. Carley said didn't she want a cup of tea. She said he would never understand anything. She said he must go away. She said the fact that he would never understand anything was the reason she liked him but also the reason he must now go away; they must both go away, all she needed was to be left alone. Hurt, Carley left her alone, slept on the sofa and in the morning left for a four day drive to Aberdeen and back. On the second day Nancy got up in the evening but took a cup of tea back to her room and stayed there. Vere heard her muttering to herself angrily and occasionally cursing (her language often surprised him). The next evening she dressed up smartly and went out. She came back very late; he knew that because she knocked over a small table on her way through the sitting room to the bedroom. The following morning she was up before him, tidying the flat and singing. By the time Carley came back in the evening all her vitality had returned. Carley's relief and pleasure reinforced Vere's own; he had never seen Carley in such a mood. The evening was a celebration of more than Nancy's return to good humour; Vere felt close to – hardly excluded from – the splendour of their love. His admiration for both increased in the light of their admiration for each other.

One day a letter came for Nancy from the Artist. She read it aloud. 'I created you', it said. 'You are my finest – no, my only – work of art. I need you, I need to look at you. Your mad bad sad desire to possess everyone on whom your wayward glance alights need not prevent that. Nancy, dear Nancy, come home to your loving Artist.' Here he had added a neat pen and ink drawing of himself. He had a small pointed beard and big eyes with tears falling out of them and down his cheeks.

Nancy read out the letter in very melodramatic tones and burst out laughing.

'If only you could know what a fraud he is! I wish you could meet him – you'd like him – he's so funny. But no one could live with him for long. He's too vain. But the worst thing is knowing all the time that nothing, but nothing, he says is ever quite true.'

Carley and Vere were embarrassed by her frankness, not sure it was right for her to be talking like this. She jumped up and kissed Carley.

'Not like you,' she said. 'Everything you say is quite, quite true. Isn't it?'

'That's because I'm not an artist,' said Carley. 'How did he know your address?'

'I wrote to him. I thought he might send me some money. He did enough pictures of me and I never charged him, did I?'

But in the morning she did not get up. When Mrs Wilson Clark, having received no response to her repeated rings on the door bell, used her master key and opened the door, she found Nancy in bed, the cup of tea Carley had left for her cold on the table beside her. Carley had taken both dogs with him because he was doing a drive he knew well, from Bath to Shepton Mallet and on to Yeovil, delivering timber, and he knew the dogs could have a good run in the woods on the way back. The flat, however, still smelt of dogs, and toast and possibly, Mrs Wilson Clark thought, tensing her nostrils, men.

Having opened the bedroom door rather dramatically – her heart beating quite fast – she waited at the foot of the bed for some reaction from its occupant. There was none. The bed was an untidy heap of bedclothes, with Carley's striped pyjamas thrown down on one side of it, and among the pillows Nancy's dark hair and white face extraordinarily exposed. Mrs Wilson Clark's heart continued to beat fast. She felt the boldness of her intrusion. She had only once before in her life done such a thing, when she had had to go into a maid's bedroom when the girl had not lit the fires and made the breakfast; it had transpired she had influenza. She had been taken away in an ambulance and later the news came that she had died; it had been in the epidemic of 1918.

'Are you ill?'

Nancy did not move or open her eyes, but said distantly, 'No.'

'I see you are not an early riser.'

Nancy opened her eyes.

'I think I am not a riser at all,' she said. Her eyes were very dark blue and looked at Mrs Wilson Clark out of her white face as if from a great distance. 'I think it much more likely I shall sink.'

'Are you in trouble?' Mrs Wilson Clark, her mind at sea, still clung to the frail notion of servant girls and their problems. 'In trouble' to her meant 'pregnant'.

'Certainly,' said Nancy calmly from the pillows. 'Certainly I am in trouble. I have . . .' She made an effort to sit up, failed, sank back weakly on the pillows, tried again and succeeded, crossed both her hands on her breast as if it hurt her to breathe. 'I have . . .' She bowed her head, shook it gently from side to side. 'I have . . . trouble . . .' She lowered her bare feet to the floor. 'Would you be very kind and pass me my dressing-gown?'

Mrs Wilson Clark detached the blue silk kimono from the hook to which Nancy's gaze directed her, and held it out. Nancy slipped it over the white silk nightdress and smiled a sad polite smile. 'Thank you.'

'Are you living here?' asked Mrs Wilson Clark, thinking it best when in doubt to attack.

'Oh no,' answered Nancy. 'I am not living here. I am not living anywhere.' She sank down on the edge of the bed. 'You shouldn't have bothered to come here. You should have sent for me. I would have come.'

'Well, I'm sure you would, yes,' allowed Mrs Wilson Clark weakly; then, rallying, she added: 'I thought it best to bring matters into the open.'

Nancy looked at her as if her attention had been really caught for the first time. An extraordinarily eager smile came onto her face.

'I *hate* secrets. More than anything I hate secrets.'

Mrs Wilson Clark smiled back.

'I know what we'll do,' said Nancy. 'You go back upstairs and I'll get dressed, and in a minute I'll come upstairs and see you and I'll tell you everything.'

That was the time Mrs Wilson Clark heard about Nancy's grandmother, the widow of the dentist in Tunbridge Wells.

*

That summer Vere introduced Nancy to bicycling and fishing. To his surprise she seemed to like them both. She made herself a pair of grey flannel shorts on Elaine's sewing machine out of Elaine's old school skirt and Elaine gave her a blue aertex shirt she said she never wore, and Nancy tied her hair back with a bandeau made out of one of Carley's red spotted handkerchiefs and Mrs Wilson Clark lent her her bicycle which she had not used for years but which Vere soon had in working order. 'It will do her good to get out a bit,' said Mrs Wilson Clark. 'Bring some roses into her cheeks.'

Elaine had gone out on the morning that her mother was supposed to have turned Nancy out of the basement flat. She had gone with a party of regular worshippers at the Church of St John the Baptist to a Prayer Meeting at Wells at which they were to be addressed by the Bishop. It was an all day meeting and included a light lunch at a cost of three shillings and sixpence. Elaine had had no intention of going until she heard of her mother's plan to confront the brazen hussy in her den of vice. She had no doubt the hussy was brazen since her mother and Mrs Behr were so sure of it, and she was very sad to hear it and to think that such things could go on in Bath of all places, but her mother was so terrifying when she was angry and had so often bent her anger upon Elaine herself that Elaine knew she was in danger of feeling sympathy for the hussy, however brazen; and since she knew her mother must be right and knew also that it was useless to resist her even when she was not right, Elaine felt the only way to avoid the succession of sleepless nights, which would certainly ensue if she were to witness any kind of face to face encounter between her mother and Nancy, was to be away from the house all day. Luckily remembering the Church excursion to Wells, she left in the morning in her hat and gloves saying, 'Oh yes, mother, don't you remember I told you I was going? The Miss Ormerods made such a thing of it.' The Miss Ormerods, who had made no more of a thing of it than to say rather half-heartedly that they thought of going themselves, were

27

surprised to see her but quite pleased; they often said to each other that poor little Elaine Wilson Clark ought to get out more.

Professor Behr, whose feelings were not unlike Elaine's, though less extreme, had spent the day at the Reference Library, making notes for his history of European culture; and it was only Hilda Behr who paused on the way up to her flat and heard the sound of voices long after she would have expected the disgraced girl to have left, bag and baggage, as the English phrase had it. Much later she came downstairs, and having knocked gently, put her head round the drawing-room door to say, 'I do so hope you were not having too unpleasant an interview?'

Mrs Wilson Clark was sitting in an armchair with some embroidery waiting for Betsy to bring her her tea. She had been dozing.

'Do come in,' she said graciously. 'But only for a moment as I have one of my heads.'

'I am so sorry. I do hope she was not insolent?'

'Life,' said Mrs Wilson Clark magisterially, 'has not been kind to that poor girl. We were able to talk about friends in common. In Tunbridge Wells.'

Hilda Behr remained in an attitude of uncomprehending enquiry.

'She is staying only temporarily,' said Mrs Wilson Clark distantly, reaching for the cigarette case on the table beside her. 'Quite temporarily.' She lit a cigarette and inhaled deeply. 'Her grandmother was a person of some standing in Tunbridge Wells.'

'Do you mean,' said Hilda Behr in surprise, 'she is a daughter of the bourgeoisie?'

'Certainly not,' said Mrs Wilson Clark to whom the word was unfamiliar. 'They were Perfectly Nice People.'

As Hilda still hesitated, half in and half out of the door, Mrs Wilson Clark waved her cigarette in a dismissive manner and said, 'Forgive me. My head.'

28

'I am so sorry. My concern was only that you had been exposed to unpleasantness.'

'No, no, no unpleasantness,' said Mrs Wilson Clark faintly, closing her eyes. It was not clear to Hilda whether she was stating a fact about the past or a hope for the future.

Opening her eyes and seeing Hilda Behr still standing anxiously by the door she added shortly, 'He is sleeping on the sofa.' She drew on her cigarette and closed her eyes again, inhaling. 'All quite temporary. Quite, quite temporary.'

Hilda Behr, though hardly satisfied, had no alternative but to leave the room.

So Nancy bicycled with Vere to the stream in which he had fished for trout since he was a small boy. They walked along the path where there were tortoiseshell butterflies sunning themselves on the heavy heads of meadowsweet and agrimony. Dragonflies hovered over the clear water in which if Vere and Nancy watched quietly they could see the dark fish moving among the weed which was elongated by the movement of the water like a girl's long hair streaming in the wind; the kingfisher's blue answered the blue of the dragonflies, cerulean or azure. Vere was a skilled fisherman, having poached trout from this stream under the eye of the Avon and Tributaries Water Authority most of his life, but when he had shown her how to do it, Nancy caught more than he did; he had never thought for a moment it could be otherwise. They took the fish home and cooked them for tea.

'They're good,' said Carley. 'You must go fishing more often.'

*

Professor Behr told Nancy she ought to see Vienna. He could not take her there. Something terrible was happening in Europe and no one in England seemed to understand or care. But Paris – had she been to Paris? No, but she knew

29

what she'd like to see there, she'd heard all about it from the Artist, she longed to see it, she knew she'd love it. Oh but Paris was made for her, he told her, all those centuries of life and love and art and beauty and ideas had existed only so that some man – 'ah my dear young lady, what man, what man?' – should be the first to show her Paris.

'You show me,' she said, daring him, in the Pump Room over morning coffee and Bath buns.

He looked at her seriously. His moustache was lightly frosted on its under edge with sugar from the bun he had just eaten. 'You have too much power. It is not safe. You know that, don't you?'

She wrinkled her nose, reached over to touch the hand with which he held his coffee cup. 'What lovely hands you have,' she said. 'So small.'

He smiled, pulled a clean white handkerchief from his top pocket releasing a hint of eau de Cologne, and wiped the sugar from his moustache. 'My feet too are unusually small for a man of my height.'

'Why doesn't Hilda like me?' she asked.

He told her that Hilda was not happy, that she had been a music teacher but had had to leave her job in a convent school in Vienna because of her Jewish ancestry. 'She took in typing so as to survive but all the time she felt so much distress at being a typist instead of a teacher, at having her head filled with my words instead of the music of Bach or Beethoven. She is always a little bit in mourning.'

'She should be with us now,' said Nancy, looking towards the platform where between potted palms the Pump Room Trio entertained the takers of tea or coffee with light music of a decorous nature for an hour or two each morning and afternoon. 'Or do you think it wouldn't quite do?'

The pianist had launched into The Lonely Ash Grove. The violinist followed tremulously, the bass player leaned over his instrument and ministered to it, in the manner of a respectful retainer plucking his sleeping master's sleeve to draw his attention to the time; he was an elderly man of deferential mien who had been painted by Sickert in 1909.

'It would do,' said Professor Behr after a moment. 'It would do. Poor Hilda.'

But quite soon poor Hilda was playing duets with Nancy on the upright Bechstein left to Mrs Wilson Clark by her mother and now in the upstairs drawing-room in the house in Henrietta Street. They played Schubert Marches. Hilda took the treble part, Nancy the bass. Hilda swayed from side to side and pounded out the music with the crisp fingering that years of writing the correct numeral over each note for less agile schoolgirls had given her. Nancy swayed beside her, providing the bass, flushed with the effort of concentration and the exhilaration induced by the idea of the happiness she was giving. Elaine sat beside her, turning the pages, her gaze fixed mostly on Nancy's face. Carley and Vere, called up to listen, looked at Nancy too. Only Professor Behr noticed that she simplified the bass part, to the extent of using no more than three chords, one of them rather haphazard; he did not care. It only made her gesture more generous, the occasion more touching.

*

When Carley came upstairs he wore a dark blue jersey. He had a suit, and the first time Mrs Wilson Clark, overcoming her social scruples, said to Nancy, 'My daughter and I would be so pleased if you would come up for a glass of sherry one evening – and do of course bring your friends,' he put it on. Nancy shrieked.

'You look so working-class.'

'I am working-class, silly.'

'No, no, there are three things that make people classless, talent, beauty, and something else I've forgotten. You have beauty.'

31

'If you say so. I don't want to upset the old basket, that's all.'

'One look from your beautiful eyes and the old basket will melt, swoon, do whatever old baskets do, unwind, unravel, turn back into a trembling reed.'

'All that if I just take off my jacket?'

But he didn't have a jersey, that first time. Later on Nancy sold one of the Artist's pictures and bought him one. That first time he wore Vere's jacket which was made of tweed and was too big for Vere because it had been passed on to him by the Vicar at his mother's instigation. Vere did have a jersey, knitted for him by his mother. Because of the many times his mother had taken Vere and Marjorie to tea at the Vicarage, Vere was more at ease in the drawing-room at Henrietta Street than Carley who had never been into a middle-class house before. Carley tended at first to stand near the door as if he were expecting to be asked to leave and when invited to sit down to move forward cautiously and sit on the edge of the chair. He was not shy. He felt that there were different rules of behaviour here, would perhaps have been disappointed had this not been so; but his wish not to transgress the rules was a wish not to offend the suscepti-bilities of the social superiors who were making friendly overtures to him; it was in no way a desire to appear as anything other than he was. Nor were his feelings towards these people deferential; he was more or less indifferent towards them. His world had been his work, his dogs, the pub, his jazz records. Cut off from an early age from his family by his distinct feeling of his difference from them, he had been content to be solitary ever since. Sex had meant a good deal to him but he had no opinion of women apart from his physical interest. Vere had been admitted into his world through the dogs, and had become as familiar as the dogs. Carley had accepted Vere; his feeling for him was fraternal, even tender, but he did not think about it because he did not name it. He named his feeling for Nancy because that was love, and everyone knew about love. If he had ever speculated as to whether or not she was the sort of girl, either temperamentally or as regards social background, that he might have been expected to have been allotted by providence as his girl, he would have seen no reason why not. He accepted her, with gratitude, with love, but without astonishment. He had therefore no feeling, when they went upstairs to the drawing room, that anyone might question his right to be there, or might think it odd that the grand-daughter of the Tunbridge Wells dentist should be consorting with the lorry-driver son of a coal miner. Nancy was his and he was Nancy's; he had given her his life. Where she went he followed, as proud of himself as of her.

*

The comic aspect of the upstairs evenings was not lost on Nancy. Downstairs, afterwards, she imitated Hilda Behr's Viennese tones and Mrs Wilson Clark's genteel banalities with some skill, and throwing herself on the sofa beside the dogs laughed extravagantly and a good deal louder than she ever laughed upstairs. Carley and Vere, though amused by this and even rather excited by it, were also sometimes embarrassed, as they were when she gave them mocking accounts of the behaviour of the Artist. They were not sure whether it was really all right to talk like that. At the same time it was irresistible; they laid aside their best behaviour and exhausted themselves in paroxysms of wild mirth at the expense of the upstairs inhabitants.

It was clear, however, that Nancy still cared for the good opinion of the household. The upstairs evenings continued, becoming gradually less formal. In an odd way too they became gradually more exciting, as the undercurrent of mockery in Nancy's sweetness came closer to the surface, and the note in her laughter which at first had only been heard downstairs, the louder note, raucous, dangerous, began to be heard in the drawing-room too.

'You laugh at us,' Professor Behr said to her sadly.

'I laugh with you,' she said. 'I am never never not with you.'

'Yes, you are generous. But as well as laughing with us you laugh at us.'

'Not at you, Professor Behr. You're too clever. you understand me too well.'

That evening Carley had brought his gramophone upstairs, at Mrs Wilson Clark's request.

'I adore jazz,' she had most unexpectedly announced.

When Elaine heard the music – it was Carley's favourite Fats Waller record – she blushed scarlet. It spoke of goodness knew what liberties. How could her mother say she liked it? Where could she possibly have heard it?

'Mugsy Spanier,' Nancy was saying. 'Do play Mugsy Spanier, Carley.'

Elaine, pale now, looked at Nancy's flushed face. She wished the music would stop. At the same time she thought how wonderful it would be if Nancy would dance.

Mrs Wilson Clark was looking puzzled. She had expected something different. Carley changed the record. '"I wish that I could shimmy like my sister Kate . . ."'

'I don't think this is what we used to play in the Club in Bombay,' said Mrs Wilson Clark.

'"Just like two jellies on a plate . . ."'

'One could hardly dance to it.'

'What dances did you dance in the Club in Bombay?' Nancy asked.

'Foxtrots, dear. Foxtrots, of course.'

'Foxtrots,' said Nancy. 'Foxtrots, Carley.'

Carley looked through the pile of records, interrupted Mugsy Spanier, put on Nat Gonella.

'Foxtrot,' he said.

Professor Behr bowed to Mrs Wilson Clark, stepped forward smartly, received her hand in his, her other hand upon his shoulder, her substantial form into his arms.

Elbows out and feet in perfect time to the music, he guided her into the middle of the drawing-room floor.

'It's fun!' cried Hilda Behr. She looked towards Carley and Vere but Carley could not dance; he was happier winding the gramophone. Vere's mother had taught him to dance; that is to say once or twice she had managed to persuade him to stump round the sitting-room with Marjorie, learning the difference between a foxtrot and a waltz and a tango; they had drawn the line at the rhumba. He stepped forward, bowed in imitation of the Professor, and began to dance with Hilda.

'Bravo!' cried Nancy, with the emphasis on the first syllable (the Artist had had an Italian friend, a painter of murals). 'Bravo!' and she stretched out her hands to Elaine.

'Oh I hardly – I really . . .' Elaine blushed but held out her hands in response. They danced. Three couples danced while Carley wound the gramophone and changed the record, pleased with the success of his music.

'Oh wait . . .' Elaine ran from the room.

Mrs Wilson Clark sat on a chair, patting her wig. Her cheeks were plum-coloured from the effects of the exercise combined with the rouge.

'Such ages since one's danced,' she said breathlessly. 'Elaine!' she added in astonishment. 'Just look at you!'

Elaine had come back into the room. She had taken all the hairpins out of her hair, which she usually wore in a loose bun; it fell in abundant brown waves well below her shoulders.

'How beautiful,' called Nancy. 'You look beautiful.' But she was dancing with Professor Behr. Elaine hesitated, looked anxiously towards her mother, but Vere asked her to dance and Nancy reached out a hand to touch her hair as she passed; and Elaine danced, her former exhaltation returning.

Another dance or two and it was all over.

'We have to go,' Nancy announced. 'Carley has to get up

at four o'clock to drive to the mysterious East. Pack up, my darlings. We're going home.'

Vere picked up the gramophone, Carley collected the records, Nancy threw her shawl around her shoulders, said goodbye, would hear no protests, laughed, smiled, left, ran back to kiss Elaine on the cheek and tell her how beautiful she was, and led the way downstairs.

In the basement she kicked off her shoes and threw herself on the sofa saying she couldn't have borne another minute of it and wasn't Mrs Wilson Clark a scream when she danced. They played the other records then and danced more wildly and the dogs who had joined in at first became sleepy and went back to their boxes, and Nancy danced on the sofa and the table, and Carley took off his jersey and danced too, a big man with his arms held out sideways and his head back, laughing, while Nancy spun and teasingly gyrated and occasionally embraced him, and Vere jigged around in the corner, perfectly happy.

*

Carley had to drive to East Anglia and was away for four days. The house in Henrietta Street was quiet in the sun; it was a quiet street. Behind the decorous fronts quiet lives went on. The respectability which Hilda Behr found so uncongenial because it was so unlike the respectability of Vienna, lay upon Henrietta Street and Laura Place and Pulteney Bridge, and draped over these quiet places a gentle monotony, a deep provincial calm. History might happen elsewhere; here Mrs Wilson Clark put on her second best hat and took her umbrella, though there was not a cloud in the sky, and went round the corner to the St John the Baptist Church Hall for a Bazaar in aid of the Church of England Missionary Society.

Vere and Nancy bicycled to the river. Sight, sound and smell conspired. So did the heat, and the fact there were no fish around on such a day.

After a time Vere folded his rod. He had been standing on a small gravel spit at the foot of a miniature cliff whose summit was about at the level of his head. A tree overhung the river. He walked towards it, intending to use its lowest branch to pull himself up the bank, and saw that Nancy was there, half concealed by the leaves.

'I've given up too. I'll come down.'

He held a hand up. She took it, reached for the other hand, slid down the bank, looked into his face; they kissed. Vere had kissed girls before, but that was all. Of this first violent consummation, to which a fold in the formation of the river bank afforded hospitality, he remembered afterwards chiefly Nancy's panting breath and her final cry; these were sounds he had not heard before. Afterwards she lay still on the grass, her eyes shut, the hair on her forehead slightly damp. Vere raised himself, moved away to sit on a half-submerged log, his head in his hands. Above the sound of the river he heard her move, climb up the bank, walk away through the long grass. He did not follow her.

Later she came and sat beside him on the log. She put her arm round his bent shoulders.

'We must go now, Vere.'

'Carley,' he groaned.

'Carley will be back.'

'What can we say to him? What can we do?'

'Nothing, Vere, nothing. There's no need.'

'No need?' He turned to look at her.

She was serene.

'Nothing's changed. And besides, Carley doesn't mind. Really. Believe me. Don't worry.'

He did not believe her. He never did believe her, quite. But he believed that she believed it. Otherwise she could not have behaved as she did, with no change that he could see in her manner to Carley and very little change when Carley was there in her manner to Vere. She told him that it made no difference, that anyway Carley did not mind that sort of thing, that only conventional stupid people thought making love with one person meant you could never make love with anyone else, that for her it was an expression of affection and of joy in life, not a tie, a bond, a means to slavery.

'I've never been possessive,' she said. 'Why should anyone be possessive about me? I could never belong completely to one person.'

'I don't know. I don't know about all that. It's too complicated. Maybe I haven't enough experience.'

'Believe me. Carley doesn't mind.'

'Does he know?'

'No. I shan't tell him. But he doesn't mind in theory. I know. We've talked about it.'

'About me? Have you talked about me?'

'No.'

He trusted her, of course. How did he know how Carley felt about matters he had never discussed with him? He did feel that if he had been Carley he would have minded; but then that could have been because he was inexperienced, not sensible as Nancy told him he should be, too conventional, which Nancy told him he should not be. The apparent return to routine reassured him, the days at work, the evenings with Nancy and Carley, the occasional visits upstairs.

Carley was away more in the summer than in the winter and on those occasions Vere and Nancy made love. The effect of this on Vere, the revelation of physical love, was overwhelming; he could no more have held back from the extraordinary delight of it than he could have forborn to breathe. He had desired her for a long time without recognizing it; now that he had recognized it he thought about it nearly all the time, dwelling on its fulfilment in recollection and in anticipation until all his life for the time being was a sensual dream of Nancy, and everything he saw or heard or touched that summer spoke to him of her.

Professor Behr told Nancy that Prague was the most beautiful city in Europe. He told her that if war came he and Hilda might be sent to a concentration camp. He showed her a piece of paper given to him by the English Home Office, a passport for the stateless. He told her that before the Great War he had travelled all over Europe and to India and America without showing anyone his passport.

'No one ever asked to see it,' he said. 'In those days one could be a citizen of the world. Now because Hitler has deprived me of my Austrian passport I am a citizen of no state. This is honourable. I am proud to be a stateless person.'

They were walking across Pulteney Bridge together, he with a pile of library books under his arm, she with the dogs on their leads. He was proud to be walking with Nancy. He was not proud to be a stateless person; that was a lie.

'We'll go to the cinema,' Nancy said. 'You like the cinema don't you? There's something good on, I can't remember what. We'll go tomorrow, just you and me, and perhaps Elaine – we'll take Elaine, to cheer her up. We'll go to the afternoon performance, and we'll have lunch together first. What about that?'

★

Summer was coming to an end. The war scare seemed to have passed; a telegram of gratitude was sent to Mr Chamberlain by the Mayor on behalf of the people of Bath. A sort of impatience seemed to have come upon Nancy, hard to define but evident to those who loved her, an occasional extra feverishness in her gaiety, an occasional extra desolation on her days of inactivity. Carley said he would take her with him on a trip to the North. It was going to take more than a week; she would be able to stop off in Edinburgh and see some of her old friends there. Nancy seized on the idea with enthusiasm and built it up into a great adventure. They would go to the Highlands, the heather would be out. She tore several of her clothes to pieces and sewed them into new ones; every evening there seemed to be a new dress to be paraded, a new arrangement of shawls or belts or shoes to be tried out on the approving Carley and Vere. Carley was pleased with the success of his idea, and began to plan for it too. He asked his employers if he could have a few days off before making the return journey south; since he had hardly ever asked for a holiday they agreed.

On an afternoon in early autumn Vere bicycled through Bath on his way home to Henrietta Street. There had been little work that day and after lunch Mr Bodman, coming over to Vere's corner of the workshop and finding him slowly re-arranging his already tidy tools, the two bicycles on which he had been working finished and waiting for collection, had unexpectedly said, 'Go home, lad, if you want to. Take the afternoon off. You've not been looking yourself lately.'

Vere had thanked him gratefully, jumped on his bicycle and set off at speed, thinking to dash back to Nancy, and set off with her to the valley with their fishing rods; but half way across Bath the heaviness of spirit which was begin- ning to become familiar to him descended. Perhaps she wouldn't want to come, perhaps if she did it wouldn't work; perhaps he ought to take the opportunity to go and see his mother, and finish splitting the logs he had collected for her over the summer. Or if he did go to Henrietta Street, and if Nancy were there alone, would they go through to the big bed and stay there until it was nearly time for Carley to come home, and would he then take the dogs out and walk round and round Henrietta Gardens and Sydney Gardens, where the leaves were beginning to turn yellow and where from time to time a train came puffing past and children ran to look at it and wave, and where his feeling of unease would be gently overlaid by a kind of all-embracing sadness, which seemed like pity for the whole world rather than for himself? He pedalled more slowly, past the Guildhall and the Imperial Hotel towards the river, and then as he approached the bridge he saw a broad back ahead of him, and a fair head held slightly back as if to look up at the sea gulls which were wheeling over the bridge because the old woman who was often there with her bag of bread crumbs had just appeared. The sight of this familiar figure, walking at a good pace along the pavement, made him accelerate, and draw up beside him with a squeak of brakes, and say, smiling, 'What are you doing here?'

'Those brakes need oiling,' said Carley.

'Bodman gave me the afternoon off. No work.'

'The lorry's in for overhaul before tomorrow. I've got to fetch it in an hour or so. I thought I'd come over and take the dogs for a walk.'

'I'll come with you.'

They walked on together, Vere wheeling his bicycle. They turned out of Laura Place into Henrietta Street. There was no one much about in the quiet afternoon. Vere leant his bicycle against the railings, then followed Carley down the steps. He heard Carley speak to the dogs, and call Nancy. The lights were not on.

'She's out,' said Carley. 'I'll get the leads. I left them in here.'

He opened the bedroom door, stood still. Vere came up behind him, and looked in. Three faces were turned towards them. Elaine lay on her back on the bed, Nancy was lying beside her raised on one elbow, Professor Behr was standing close to them on the other side of the bed. All three of them were naked. Elaine looked at Carley and Vere as though she were in a trance, Professor Behr, whose hands had flown to protect his private parts, looked at them as if they were the death squad he had been expecting, Nancy was flushed and bright-eyed; her expression was fiercely defiant.

Carley turned, pushed Vere to one side, and ran out of the flat. The dogs followed him. Vere followed the dogs.

In Henrietta Gardens Carley paused to allow Vere to catch up with him. They were both short of breath from running.

'Leave me alone,' said Carley.

'I can't.'

'I've got to be alone. Hold the dogs.'

'You'll come back?'

Carley walked quickly away. Vere held the dogs by their collars and watched him go.

★

Mrs Wilson Clark arranged the funeral. The Vicar of the Church of St John the Baptist, round the corner from Henrietta Street in St John's Road, was hesitant; suicide was a sin. Mrs Wilson Clark overruled him. Suicide was neither here nor there she said; Carley had died as a result of liver failure.

'But I understood . . . I mean . . .' said the Vicar. 'Was there not . . . poison?'

'That was on quite a separate occasion,' said Mrs Wilson Clark.

It was true, in the sense that Carley had drunk the weed-killer in the early hours of the morning after Vere had last seen him, having forced the lock of the gardeners' shed in Henrietta Gardens, and had died two days later because the poison which had been pumped out of him in hospital soon after he was discovered by a railway worker walking across the park at dawn had had time to destroy his liver, so that strictly speaking he could be said to have died from the after-effects of a suicide attempt rather than in the course of a suicide attempt. The Vicar allowed himself to be satisfied with this explanation partly because he was afraid of Mrs Wilson Clark who was a prominent member of his not very large congregation, and partly because he had long ceased to

42

worry about the finer points of religious observance. You had to have a Church and you had to have Vicars, that was about the extent of his faith nowadays, and he would have been hard put to it even to say why these things were necessary; he certainly did not think that any importance should be attached to the manner in which their functions were performed.

So he mumbled and rushed his way through the funeral service, and Vere hardly listened, looking round the dim and half-empty Church at the men who had worked with Carley, and at Mr and Mrs Bodman and the stricken household from Henrietta Street (apart from Nancy, who hated funerals she said) and Carley's family, found and informed by the police, uncomfortable in their funeral clothes and guilty because Carley had been a mystery to them, ashamed because it seemed he'd brought them into disrepute by killing himself, drinking poison in a public park at dead of night in order by inflicting unspeakable pain on himself to destroy a greater pain at whose nature they could not, and would not, guess.

At some point the congregation sang, 'Abide with me'. Vere noticed that no one needed a hymn-book; they knew the words by heart. They sang them loudly, trailing behind the organist. 'The darkness deepens; Lord with me abide.' The family, staring straight in front of them, droned out the words without expression; but others among the congregation put back their heads and sang with feeling, swooping with doleful emphasis from one note to another, ignoring the organist's attempts to speed them along.

> 'Swift to its close ebbs out life's little day;
> Earth's joys grow dim, its glories pass away . . .'

The fact that everyone knew the words made it seem to Vere a ceremony, and therefore proper, a way in which

Carley's death could be marked as it should be, by an understood ritual.

When the Vicar began to speak again Vere's now awakened attention wandered away from the prayers, although the sound of them underlay his thoughts and the occasional word penetrated his consciousness, and he found himself presented with a sudden clear surprising picture of Carley on the hospital bed where he had last seen him, but upright now and apparently weightless though still with that extraordinary pallor and stiffness; and this figure floated up from the bed and passed easily through the ceiling and the roof into the sky above Bath, and as he rose above the city a company of fiercely beautiful beings streamed from a great height to meet him. Vere tried to hold on to this picture but it faded from his mind's eye. He gripped the front of the pew, and trembled, and said quite loudly through his clenched teeth, 'They'd better, they'd bloody better.' Mrs Wilson Clark touched his arm and said, 'Come along, dear. Time to stand up now.'

*

Nancy hated funerals, she said. She'd said she hated fuss, the evening Carley disappeared.

'Don't fuss,' she said to Vere. 'He'll be back.'

Vere had held the dogs by their collars until Carley had been out of sight long enough to be sure they would not follow him. Then he walked them round the garden, threw sticks for them aimlessly, seemed only able to think how amazing it was that the whole thing should have gone so quickly to his stomach, which was in turmoil.

When he eventually returned to the flat he found Nancy sitting alone on the sofa with a bottle of German wine beside her and a glass in her hand.

'He'll be back,' she said. 'Don't fuss.'

She did not look at him. Perhaps because of the wine, her face had an expression that was not familiar to him, dazed and at the same time sated, a rather stupid look. As the night progressed the look disappeared; he never saw it again. It was replaced by an expression which was familiar, the expression she wore on the days when she didn't get up; the mouth turned down at the corners, the eyes ringed with shadow; those were the days on which it seemed there was nothing anyone could do for her. Towards dawn she got up from the sofa and packed a suitcase full of the clothes she had been preparing to take to Scotland. Vere, who had been out to search the streets for Carley, came in just as she was carrying it into the sitting-room.

'I'm going to bed,' she said. 'Tell him not to wake me when he comes in.'

Vere had thought for a moment he had seen Carley, walking slowly by the river in front of the old prison with his hands in his pockets, but by the time Vere reached the place the man had gone. It might have been Carley. It appeared later that he had spent most of the night aimlessly walking, and had only broken into the shed and drunk the poison an hour or so before he was found. It was never clear whether he had known the weed-killer was there or whether he had guessed it might be or whether he had been looking for something else. He was not able to speak in the hospital, though on the second day he was semi-conscious. Vere sat beside him for as much of the time as the Sister would let him, after the policeman whose bicycle he kept in repair – the one who had been sent for by Mrs Wilson Clark on the day when she thought Carley and Vere and the dogs were fighting – had called to tell them where he was. Once Carley turned his head on the pillow and looked at Vere; Vere looked into his eyes and begged him to get better and thought he saw a response, a softening of his gaze, an echo of a smile. In the morning the sister said, 'He went in the night. We didn't know where to find you.'

*

When Vere came back from the funeral Nancy, who had been in bed when he had left, was up and dressed, one of her shawls round her shoulders, held in place at her neck by a big brooch of Cairngorm stones which the Artist had given her.

'We're off.' Her face was smooth, youthful, delicately flushed with excitement at the prospect of a journey, untouched by grief or doubt.

'Where to?'

'Scotland of course. I wrote to my friends. They were expecting me yesterday. Come on.'

'What do you mean, come on?'

'I've been to the station and got the tickets. It'll be fun.'

'Fun?'

'Vere, we have to live. Carley said so. He said if anything happened I was to be happy. He said I was to stay with you. Stay with Vere, he said.'

'I don't believe you. I don't believe Carley said those things.'

The dogs, impatient to get going, were fussing round the door.

'Vere, would I lie to you? To you, Vere?'

Rosie let out a short high bark; Bess jumped against the door. Nancy dashed at the door and pulled it open.

'Bloody dogs. Vere, listen, I need you, don't you understand? You can't leave me?'

'The road,' said Vere. They never let the dogs out without first making sure the road was clear. He started up the steps. 'Oh Christ.' A squeal of brakes, a bump, a yelp, silence. A car door opened. Vere ran up the steps to see Rosie lying on the road. A car had stopped. A man stood awkwardly; two other people were approaching. Rosie moved, tried to stand, failed. Nancy ran past him, sat on the road, her arms around Rosie. She looked over Rosie's head to Vere.

'I'll stay with her. We'll both stay. We have to now.'

She had looked at Elaine like that, the evening Elaine let down her hair.

Vere took Bess by the collar and bundled her down the steps. He grabbed the box that held his savings from by his bed, shut Bess in, carried his bicycle up the steps, jumped on it, shouted, 'I'm going for the vet.' He sped through the side streets to Mr Higgins, flung into his surgery. 'Go at once,' he said. 'There's no one but Nancy.' He saw Mr Higgins pick up his bag. He knew Mr Higgins had fallen for Nancy the day Rosie cut her leg on a piece of glass in the park and had to have four stitches. He jumped on his bicycle again and rode as furiously as before to the station. The London train was in. He dashed up the stairs with the bicycle, friendly hands helped him, pushed the bike in the guards van. The train moved, he found a seat, felt in his pockets for his sister's address. The stone terraces of Bath began to slide past the window. It was over.

*

He never went back to Bath, even when his mother died. He drove over to the village from Salisbury Plain to see her in her last illness. It was wartime by then, and he was in the Army. His sister Marjorie went into the Wrens and married a sailor. Vere didn't marry; he would say when asked that it just hadn't turned out that way.

He became a sergeant, and a notable rugger player, in the Army, and after the War he took a job at a boys' boarding school not far from London, as a rugger coach and fitness training expert. Perhaps the Army had given him a taste for institutional life, for he found the work congenial and the boys cheerful. The place had not traditionally been a rugger school, and he made it one. After matches the team would take him to a pub. After a victory the richer boys sometimes bought champagne. They pressed it on him with a combination of condescension and eagerness to be liked and just occasionally a wonderfully open-hearted affection. He lived in a small house by the river and had two Alsatian dogs.

One day in the spring of 1959 he was in London, walking down the King's Road, when he saw Nancy. It was twenty years since he had last seen her. He had had lunch with an old Army friend who had started a small private gymnasium not far from Sloane Square; he had gone back to the gym with him after lunch and watched some young men from a London rowing club lifting weights. The pavements of the King's Road were crowded with young people encouraged by the weak and still wintry sunshine to dress for spring. Some of the girls were extraordinarily pretty with fringes and long hair and big surprised eyes flattered by make-up. Having a little time to fill in before his train left Paddington, Vere began to walk up the King's Road looking idly at the shop windows and the passers-by. Through the casually dressed crowd he saw a woman approaching him whose aspect spoke of Bond Street rather than Chelsea. She wore a coat of black Persian lamb, very high-heeled shoes, a large hat of some soft greyish fur flecked with white; she looked elegant and out of place. Her face was calmly beautiful, expressionless, perfectly made-up. She might have been a ballet dancer, a star perhaps, taking care of herself in order to sustain a career of astonishingly long duration. As she passed him he stared at her, and received in return a glance of the coldest hauteur. He recognized Nancy.

He hesitated, wondering if he could be wrong; then turned and followed her, determined to make sure. Just before reaching Sloane Square, she turned into Peter Jones. He followed her into the linen department. She asked for two dozen Irish linen table napkins. Her voice was as it had always been.

'I'd like to put that down on my account.'

The assistant's pencil hovered.

'P – A – ?'

'It's a Greek name. I'll write it for you shall I?'

An address in Mount Street. That would be the London flat; then there would be the house in the country, and something in the South of France, and of course the yacht. He might have known that that would be what she would have done, being no longer young; she would have married a Greek shipowner. The questions which had rushed suddenly into his mind when he first recognized her faded. There was nothing to be said.

He walked to the underground. He bought an evening paper and read it on his way to Paddington. At Paddington he was in good time for his train. Settling back into his seat, he smiled at his own lack of curiosity. She had survived, that was all. He was glad of that. He had survived himself, just about.

Distant Cousins

Tuscany is a big place; it extends from the Appenines to the Tyrrhenian Sea, from the mountains north of Florence to the low hills and broad valleys of the Umbrian border; if I say that something took place in Tuscany I am giving nothing away.

When you leave the main roads you find an infinitely complex network of dusty unmade-up tracks linking the many hundreds of farmhouses, hamlets, abandoned schoolhouses, seldom-used churches and small isolated dwellings which hardly justify the name of farmhouse, which scatter that beautiful and long-civilized land. One of these last my wife and I acquired twenty years ago, when prices were lower and hopes were higher; I was going to be a real writer in those days. The house is square and more or less featureless; the colours of the stones of which it is built are the colours of the earth and rock on which it stands. We bought it for the view, which extends for miles over vineyards, olive groves, farmhouses, woods of scrubby oak and arbutus, cypress and the occasional sweet chestnut, as far as the towers of – well, Tuscany is full of towers – and the distant metal-bearing mountains which separate us from the sea.

We made few alterations to the house, except to put in some plumbing and whitewash the inside walls; later on we decided it was too dangerous to rely on oil lamps – we were drinking a lot at the time and tended to knock them over – so we paid the vast sum required to bring us electricity. As I say, it was for the view that we bought the house, although I must admit that now it sometimes seems to me one of the most completely satisfactory buildings in the world. I have spent a good deal of time there alone, in the spring and autumn usually – it is too cold in the winter – and I have grown fond of it. Things have changed in Tuscany since we first went there. The country is more prosperous. The wine trade is flourishing; the terraces which had been there since pre-Roman times have been bulldozed away so that the vineyards can be maintained by machine. Sentimental foreigners regret this, but it has brought prosperity to those who have remained on the land – many left during the years of the 'Italian miracle' when agriculture was a despised way of life and there was easy money to be made in the towns. Sentimental foreigners abound in Tuscany. I never see them. I go there to work. I am known in the village and left alone. The influx of tourists and foreign residents has made my local villagers richer but it has not taken away their respect for other people's individuality, that peculiarly civilized characteristic which makes me even now look on those people, whom generally speaking I know only by their Christian names (and sometimes even those turn out to be unofficial – they are great ones for nicknames) and with whom my relationship, though easy, is not familiar, with something closer to love than any emotion I now feel for anyone else. In other words, I am a sentimental foreigner too.

It was in July that the strange thing happened. I have not been there since. I had spent most of the spring in Tuscany and had not meant to go back there until the autumn. It was because of Bettina that I found myself there in July, though whether because she had threatened to go there herself if the house was empty or because she had told me in her usual overbearing way that I must produce a new book by the autumn so that I could take it to her lover's wife's agent who would be much better than my own, I am unable to say. Most of my encounters with Bettina these days lead me in to a maze of mixed motives; probably they always have. Since

our divorce twelve years ago, Bettina has become a successful antique dealer. She is an intensely animated, amusing
and to most people, I imagine, attractive person. She is not
attractive to me because her very existence is a reproach to
me; there can be no doubt I failed her as a husband more
than she could possibly be said to have failed me as a wife –
and also even now I have a slight fear in the back of my mind
that she might pounce on me. I should be terrified. I am a
heterosexual, though youth's ardours I suppose have some-
what faded, but Bettina – well, those scars never quite heal –
when we were quarrelling badly we said such terrible things
to each other. But she's attractive, as I say, to other people,
and has a lover called James who is pompous and correct,
very generous to her and married to a best-selling novelist.
He himself is a successful barrister, specializing, I think, in
income tax affairs. He and his wife make a great deal of
money between them and spend a great deal of time making
dispositions about it. James has given Bettina much useful
advice about her business and indirectly James' wife has
given a good deal of advice to me about mine.

Bettina rang me up in June: 'Arabella says have you
changed your agent?'

'Arabella?'

'You know perfectly well who I mean.'

James' surname is Wood, but his wife writes Regency
romances under the name of Arabella de Forrest. She
employs two research assistants and the ghastly thing about
what she produces is that it really isn't too bad.

'She's told this man about you. He's expecting to hear
from you. Why haven't you done anything about it?'

'Pride. It doesn't seem to me appropriate that my ex-
wife's lover's wife should be patronising me in this way.'

'It's nothing to do with pride. It's just laziness. Besides
she doesn't know anything about James and me.'

'I know about James and you. You know about James
and you. James presumably knows about James and you.'

'You're prevaricating. Do do something about it. It's for your own good. You know old Pope is hopeless.'

'I've been with Phil Pope for twenty years. Besides I can't go to another agent without another book. I need to start with a new book. New book, new agent. That's the only way I can do it.'

'Write another book then.'

'I can't, just like that.'

'Of course, you can. Do another Scobie book. You know you can always turn those out in a flash. Anyway try. And another thing. If you aren't going to be in the house in Tuscany in the summer, do you think James and I might take it from you for a few weeks? He'd pay you a huge rent.'

'He'd hate it.'

'No, he loves simple things. And he knows that part of Italy well and speaks perfect Italian. July, I thought, or the beginning of August.'

'I'll let you know.'

Bettina and James Wood in my house, taking possession, Bettina with her wiry black hair, James knowing that part of Italy well and speaking perfect Italian – it seemed an appalling idea to me. At the same time she was right in saying that I could always turn out a Scobie book. Scobie is a space traveller who has thoroughly corny science fiction adventures accompanied by his dog Rameses whom he found in an Egyptian tomb and who has strange powers. They have attracted a modest following and are in fact my bread and butter; I have no cake. The books are not really very satisfactory because I have an unscientific mind and the details of the extra-terrestial places these two visit and of the various means of transport they use to reach these places and the various life-support systems they evolve in order to survive in them, bore me. I work out the outline and then I get my friend Harvey Brean who works at the Science Museum in Kensington to fill in the technical bits. It doesn't work awfully well and it means I have to pay him a third of my royalties, but it's a system that seems to have become established over the years; we have produced ten Scobie stories so far and there seems no reason why we should not go on indefinitely.

When Bettina telephoned to ask whether I had made up my mind about letting the house to James Wood, I told her that I had decided to go there myself to write without interruption and produce a Scobie book within a couple of months so as to have something to show the new agent in the autumn. She said she quite understood, sounding hurt.

*

It was hot, but not as hot as it sometimes is in July. Most days a breeze from the West began to blow about mid-day and in the evening it was cool enough to walk. I worked all day, and in the evenings walked miles along the dusty roads over the hills and through the woods and past the vineyards and olive groves, returning later through the pinkish evening light which quickly turned to dusk and then to night, an immense night, full of stars. I wrote on the terrace, sitting in the shade. Sometimes a tractor rattled its way steadily all day through the rows of vines on the hillside opposite, spraying; sometimes a group of five or six men and women would appear between the vines, pruning, and the sound of their conversation would reach me clearly though they were half a mile away; sometimes one of the peasants in the house whose roof I can just see to the left of my view would shout across to someone in the house which forms a group with a scarcely used chapel on the right of my view. 'Oh!' they shout and their voices carry easily across the intervening distance, 'Oh!' and then some message I can't usually make out. Often there is no human sound at all – most noticeably no traffic sound – only the distant clucking or crowing of my neighbours' hens, the occasional loud musical whistle of the golden orioles who favour the mulberry tree, the little spiralling songs of the warblers who prefer the olive trees, the rustle of a lizard over a dry leaf on the terrace, the croak of a frog from the irrigation pond by the well, the faint rustle of the poplars far down the hill by the almost dried-up bed of the stream. At noon even these sounds quieten, even the cicadas fall silent; an hour or two later the cypress trees by the chapel begin to stir; you can hear the breeze approaching over the olive trees, it reaches the chestnut tree by the terrace, a window bangs in the house. If I have written enough words for the day by then, I sometimes sleep, and in the evenings set out for my walk.

Often that July I could not allow myself to sleep. I had set myself a target of 2,000 words a day and I found it difficult to keep to it. What I can't seem to make Bettina understand is that it's as difficult to write badly as it is to write well. It's in the conception of the thing that the difference lies, not in the physical labour of getting it down on paper. To write 2,000 words of commonplace prose about lifeless characters involved in uninteresting and unlikely adventures is as hard a slog as producing 2,000 words of *War and Peace* – at least I think it is; I suppose I have never experienced the latter, although I used to fancy I was doing something very like it. The trouble with the Scobie books is that I have come to have an intense dislike for Jock Scobie. He's a red-haired extrovert, practical, unflappable, a useful man in a tight spot, about as interesting a personality as a Ford Cortina. The conversations he has with his girl-friend Eileen are of a banality that can hardly be credited – I suppose one Ford Cortina might possibly exchange such chat with another Ford Cortina should they happen to find themselves side by side in the same garage. Eileen keeps herself very fit; she teaches gym in an exclusive girls' school in between her trips to outer space with Scobie. I expect she doubles as an Under Matron too; she has very hygienic attitudes. She also has nerves of steel, an unexpectedly vigorous handshake and an apparently unlimited willingness to submit to Scobie's vile desires at any time of the day or night and in any part of the universe. Once she had a headache but my agent said the fans wouldn't like it. The fans are not so many that we can afford to treat them lightly. I deleted the headache.

Rameses is the one I like, the Egyptian dog, but it seems he's not particularly popular with the fans; they think he's too clever by half. I imagine Scobie fans are among the less sophisticated of Sci-Fi addicts; they identify with Jock and Eileen and not with Rameses. They don't mind his extra-sensory perceptions; it's the way he talks they can't stand. I suppose if Pope would only agree to it, I could push the whole thing just one step further towards farce and Rameses would become a kind of Jeeves of outer space; but no one likes that idea. It has to remain a secret between Rameses and me as to just how much that dog knows.

Even though my deadline this time was a self-imposed one, I was determined to keep to it. I have always kept to deadlines. At the same time, I found myself increasingly haunted by thoughts of other books, better books, nagged by grander concepts, drawn by half-forgotten dreams, tears, significances, hopes, glories. All that's a path down which I must not go, it's for people who have the true shaping spirit of the imagination – that spirit Coleridge lost and I never had – but there's something about that place that now and then makes the half-formed prefiguration of it that I was born with stir. It's just the quiet, I suppose, the absence of jarring interruptions, the absolute physical pleasantness of everything, the space. Every little encounter whether in the village or on my walks is pleasurable – it has something strange in it, because this is a foreign country, it has something attractively human about it, because it is on a simple level and these people are Italians, it has about it always something – something quite spurious I know because it comes only from within me – but something which seems to mean more than it does, something which speaks to the imagination.

I had my deadline to keep to. I amused myself a little as I wrote by thinking of the things Rameses might have done had he and I had our way; and one day after a particularly satisfactory morning's work, I went for a longer walk than usual and got lost.

I had a map; but the circumambulations of those white roads seem to be beyond the powers of even the most meticulous map-makers. I had been distracted too by the sight of a large bird of prey which was unfamiliar to me and which I had followed as best I could in its slow silent glide over the sloping woods, hurrying down whichever path seemed closest underneath it in an attempt to keep it in sight, until at length it slid away sideways down a current of air and disappeared rapidly behind the trees. In all the time I watched it, it made not one single wing beat; it simply rode upon the air, the spread pinions at the end of its broad wings visibly though minutely changing their positions in relation to one another in response to the wind and in the exercise of perfect control. They seemed white, these wings, or nearly white, and the chest and underparts of the bird seemed white too, lightly speckled with brown; only the short spreading tail which was moving slightly so as to perform the same steadying function as the wings, was barred with a darker colour; and though I told myself it was probably a honey buzzard, of which I knew there were some in the district, it was larger and paler than any honey buzzard I had seen before and seemed to have a wider wing span. A long time later when I remembered to look it up, I decided it could have been a short-toed eagle. But that, as I say, was later; at the time it was unknown, and marvellous.

After it had disappeared, I continued on the path along which I had been following it, but it not reappear. I was on a dusty road between small trees, looking over slopes covered with vines and patches of woodland, and the occasional tall cypress or neat olive grove, but I could see no familiar landmark. I seemed to be higher than I had ex-

60

pected and when I came upon a turning which led downhill I took it, and followed the track through the trees towards a bend beyond which I could not see. As I rounded the bend, the path narrowed and I walked between neat stacks of recently cut logs. The smell of sap mingled with that of the curry herb which grew beside the road. Someone had been thinning out the woods to good effect; there was firewood to last through the coldest of winters. There was the sound of an axe somewhere ahead of me and as I rounded another corner a tree trunk barred my way. Beyond it the track came to an end in front of a house.

It was a small stone house which backed up against the hillside, so that I was looking at the side of it, a side which was mainly taken up by a doorway surrounded by a profusion of vines growing over and around a kind of rough pergola. The front of the house faced over a small steep valley from which came the sound of falling water and a rustle of leaves from the poplars by the stream and from the plantation of sweet corn half way down the hill. The two upstairs windows which faced me as I clambered over the fallen tree and approached the house had their reddish-brown shutters closed against the evening sun. There was an extraordinary variety of plants beside the path and on the doorstep. They grew in every kind of receptacle, terracotta pots and wine jars, painted buckets, drinking troughs, an old white china sink, an enamel chamber pot, a tin bowl painted with red flowers; there were geraniums, pelargoniums, nasturtiums, white daisies, pink petunias, alyssum and aubretia spreading from their containers on to the low stone wall by the path, cacti and succulents of many different kinds, Morning Glory twining in and out of the vines round the door. The effect was both charming and comical; I found myself smiling as I approached the house. A dog barked, once, from above the road. It was a brown and white pointer, the sort you see in eighteenth century sporting prints; it watched me, wagging its stumpy tail, from an enclosure beside a hen-run. The hens and muscovy ducks clucked fussily. I looked round for the wielder of the axe I had heard earlier. He came from behind the nearest pile of logs and stood looking at me in silence.

He was a tall man, white-haired. I could not see the expression on his face because the sun, low now because it was late in the evening, was behind him. Perhaps because of this or because he had appeared so silently and now stood without moving, I felt afraid. I was surprised by my own fear, which was irrational and momentarily overwhelming, as if I had been suddenly confronted by a bear. I forced myself to move, and approached him.

'Good evening,' I said in my indifferent Italian. 'I seem to have lost my way. I was going for a walk.'

He answered me in an unexpectedly high though resonant voice, speaking with hesitation as if he had a speech impediment. He said he would ask his cousin, who was in the house. His cousin knew the roads around here better than he did.

'Come,' he said politely, gesturing towards the door.

From the inside of the house it was immediately apparent that these were not peasants. I was led into a book-lined room looking over the valley, and had time to notice how pleasantly it was furnished, with comfortable chairs, a big fruitwood table which looked more French than Italian and faded Persian rugs of a pattern I had not seen before on the floor. A man in late middle-age – the cousin – was sitting reading, with a half-empty bottle of wine beside him.

He rose to his feet and my unease vanished. The preliminaries were quickly dealt with. He was an American composer, he lived here all the time; he had done so for ten years. His name was Milton Cauldwell. He thought perhaps he had seen me in the village. He did not go out much except for the shopping; his cousin had not been well.

'You met Hal.' He indicated the man I had first seen, who

had left the room but now returned with another bottle of wine and a glass.

I introduced myself and held out my hand. Hal put down the bottle and glass. I noticed that the hand he held out to me seemed unusually long and thin – in fact the thumb, which rested briefly on the top of my hand, was longer than the average finger – but the smile with which he accompanied the gesture was a smile of such extraordinary friendliness and understanding that I immediately forgot my initial alarm. He was not so tall as I had thought. It was rather that his head was big – or not so much big as long; he had a very high forehead, but narrow, such as I have seen occasionally among Greeks or Turks. His skin on the other hand was fair, and together with the cast of his features made one think that his hair before it turned white might have been fair also – and yet he did not look Anglo-Saxon. I put him down as American of mixed ancestry; perhaps there was some Russian there, I thought. He spoke English with a Europeanized American accent, like his cousin, and with the hesitant slurr which I had noticed before.

I congratulated him on his wood collecting, and after he had sat with us a little while, not drinking but entering into the conversation in a friendly manner, he said he would like to go back to it.

'Before the light goes,' he explained apologetically. He was so polite himself that I stood up to say goodbye to him, shaking him by the hand again.

'He has had a slight stroke,' said Milton Cauldwell, when he had left the room.

I wanted to say that a stroke did not usually leave people with only four fingers on their right hand – that is to say, three fingers and a thumb – but I did not quite trust my own observation. The wine after all was strong, a good Chianti made locally from their own grapes, Cauldwell had told me.

'I'm sorry to hear it,' I said instead. 'He looks so well.'

'His mind has gone,' said Cauldwell looking enormously sad. It occurred to me that the wine had had its effect on him too.

'I should never have thought so,' I said truthfully.

'You didn't know him before.'

He sighed, and was silent.

'Look here, I really must go. You've been so kind. Just tell me again, back to the other road, on down the hill, left did you say, then right after the wood and then I shall see the church I know . . .'

'Did you ever come across a fellow called Harvey Brean in London?'

'Of course. I know him well.'

'You do? Isn't that wonderful. What could have made me ask? Now do tell me about good old Harvey.''

He had thrown off his brief depression in a moment, and revealed for the first time the exile's longing for news of the world he has left. Did I know so-and-so too, and so-and-so, friends of Harvey's? Had Harvey married, what was his work? I told him Harvey was divorced like me, possibly lonely sometimes like me, drank a bit, found satisfaction in his work.

'I taught him you know,' said Cauldwell. 'He was very bright indeed.'

'At music?' I was astonished.

'No, no, biology. I taught him biology. I was a professor of genetics at Harvard. He was one of my brightest pupils.'

'He helps me with my work. That's why I see so much of him. I write trash, that's how I make my living, science fiction and so on. Harvey fills in the technical bits. I don't know the first thing about science.'

'Scobie. You write the Scobie books. I thought your name was familiar. I've read one or two of them.'

'Good Lord. I mean, they're frightful rubbish.'

'Yes but wait a minute, there was one, I think I've got it here somewhere, you mean Harvey helped you with that?'

He began to look hurriedly along his shelves, evidently a good deal excited. 'It was about this other species, not Homo Sapiens. Descended from Homo Erectus they were.'

'*Scobie and the Other Ape.* One of the worst.'

'Well yes but you know there were one or two things in it that were quite interesting. That was Harvey, I suppose, extrapolating from what he knew. But he was wrong more often than he was right. I'm surprised he didn't make a better guess, being Harvey. Here it is, *Scobie and the Other Ape.*'

I groaned.

'No but he was on the right lines in certain ways. He was right to put most of the differences down to the brain, but it's not brain size so much as structure. The size is bigger but not all that much bigger. The structure is totally different.' He was looking through the rather grubby paperback (it certainly looked as if it had been much-read), leafing through the pages quickly looking for some particular passage he was after. A scrap of paper fell out of the book and I bent to pick it up.

'There were the fingers of course,' he was saying. 'Funny your not noticing them when you'd written it yourself.'

I looked at the piece of paper I had picked up. It was a newspaper cutting, yellow with age. It showed a photograph of a group of men posing solemnly for the camera. The ones on the left were taller and wore thick cloaks, those on the right were smaller and wore overcoats; they all wore fur hats. The ones on the left had high foreheads, long thin noses and, as far as I could see from the faded photograph, the same intelligent and expressive glance as Hal's; among the ones on the right I seemed to make out a younger Milton Cauldwell. There was writing underneath the photograph but I could not read it, because it was in Russian.

'All these gadgets,' Cauldwell was saying. 'I can see Harvey would have had fun making them up but they were quite unnecessary. They didn't need gadgets. It was all built in.'

I put down my empty glass and walked towards the window. The particular pinkish light of Tuscan evening lit the quiet valley. I thought I would go, leave this failed professor to his wine and his fantasies. Instead I said, 'Will you please explain to me, quite slowly and simply, exactly what it is you are trying to say.'

*

When later on, back in London, I told Harvey Brean about all this, he said at once, 'Milton Cauldwell. I remember him well. Not that I'd say I knew him exactly. I don't think anyone really knew Milton Cauldwell. He was a remote sort of chap. The thing was, this was in the 'fifties, the height of the McCarthy period. He had Russian friends. He knew about Russian experiments in genetics – the sort of thing you couldn't find in any Western scientific journal. We'd ask him how he knew and he'd just say he knew the people concerned, had worked with them in the war, spoke a bit of Russian, all quite open and easy – and yet somehow he wasn't the sort of person you went on asking. I never heard him talk about politics but as I say it was America, and McCarthy was on the rampage, and somehow you tended to think that anyone who was on speaking terms with a Russian must be a Communist. When he didn't come back one semester in my last year, I just assumed he'd got out, gone to Europe as so many of them did, until all that hysteria had burned itself out. I suppose most of us assumed the same thing but no one knew for certain. We were never told anything officially and as I say, he hadn't any really close friends that I knew of.'

That would have been in 1955, in the summer. According to the story Milton Cauldwell told me that evening in Tuscany, he had not gone to Europe; he had gone to Russia. He had not gone for political reasons, but on a scientific

66

expedition. He had had every intention of being back at his University in time for the start of the autumn academic term.

The man he knew was a biologist called Voroshylov. They had met during the war, both very young men on the staffs of their respective Generals on the strength of their languages – Cauldwell's maternal grandparents were first generation immigrants from Russia and he had learnt the language as a child. Voroshylov spoke several languages, including English. The two had quickly discovered their identity of interests; they had both been trained as biologists, and both hoped to do research after the War. They had kept intermittently in touch, in spite of the Cold War, and then in 1955 had come this message from Voroshylov – 'If you can by any possible means get here, come. We have an expedition in Siberia this summer which would astonish you.'

Of course he went; he was still a young man. A friend in the American Embassy in Moscow had somehow made it possible for him to get a visa. Once he was in Moscow, Voroshylov had dealt with that side of things. Voroshylov had come down from Siberia to meet him, and the day after his arrival they took the train to join the expedition.

Siberia, it seems, is not all, or not always, frozen waste. Apparently parts of the south-east are not unlike Canada, and equally rich in natural resources. It was towards the south-east that Cauldwell was taken, somewhere not far from the Chinese border. I looked the place up on the map afterwards. There are rivers there, and a range of high mountains, the Great Kinghan. Somewhere beyond the Great Kinghan the Ingodá river and the Onón join to make the Shilka; the Shilka and the Argun join to make the Amur, and the Amur joins the Sungari to flow north eastward into the Tartar Straits, that is to say into the Pacific. The valley to which Milton Cauldwell was taken was the valley of a tributary of the upper Amur. This tributary rushes down steep mountains to join the larger river; on either side of the torrent are thickly-wooded cliffs, sometimes as high as two thousand feet above the water. The last part of the journey up the gorge was made on foot, with pack ponies.

The expedition to which Voroshylov was attached was investigating that part of Siberia with a view to its eventual development by the Russian Government. Someone in the Kremlin at that time apparently thought it worth going into the possibilities of expanding in the East rather than in the West; we may regret that he changed his mind, or lost his job, or whatever it was that befell him. To this expedition were attached geographers, geologists, soil experts, anthropologists and goodness knows what else besides; it was an unwieldy collection, Cauldwell said, and Voroshylov was full of complaints. Voroshylov himself had joined the expedition out of a sense of adventure; he was supposed to be pronouncing upon the possibilities of growing different strains of wheat in the river valleys. He had written to Cauldwell because of a certain tribe they had come across, in a high valley watered by the tributary of the upper Amur; he had thought they were more interesting than anyone else in the expedition had yet understood.

I had to piece together what Cauldwell told me about this tribe, and about the valley, and his first impressions of the place. He said that he had never spoken of it with anyone else after the end of the expedition, and having started to talk he seemed to want to unburden himself of the whole thing. He had so much to say that he found it hard to organize his thoughts. I kept going back to things he had left unexplained, asking him questions, making him repeat himself. It was very late by the time I left. When it was dark Hal came in, lit the oil lamps which in our absorption we had neglected to do, and busied himself in the kitchen.

'We can talk in front of him,' said Cauldwell. 'He has forgotten it all.'

'Forgotten?'

'I'll come back to that.'

But Hal simply brought bowls of vegetable soup to the table and left them there, with bread, salami and salad. He would take his upstairs, he said, would listen to some music before going to bed. He said goodnight in his hesitant polite way and smiled his extraordinary benefaction of a smile.

'Have you found a battery record-player that's any good?' I asked when he had gone and as we went towards the table to eat. 'That was the one thing we missed before we had electricity. One can't get any of the decent music stations on the radio in these parts, can one?'

'I compose with the piano,' said Cauldwell dismissively. 'That's all I need.'

'I meant Hal. He said he was going to listen to music.'

'His music is silent. He reads it, if you like. But let me go on with what I was telling you.'

This valley then, high in the mountains, was quite wide, it seems, and unexpectedly green.

The place had been more or less mapped, of course, though not until the early years of this century, but some of the high valleys, though it was known which way they ran, had been left as suppositions; the mountainous part of the region, being thickly forested as well as steep, was difficult to move about in.

The interest of the leaders of the expedition had been aroused by rumours they had heard in the few sparse settlements around the lower part of the Shilka and the upper part of the Amur. The Chinese, they had been told, were making experiments somewhere in the border country – what sort of experiments? – weapons, the villagers said, space ships, something of that kind – lights had been seen. It was all much too vague to be taken quite seriously, but it was strange that in more than one village people spoke of these lights. The astronomers became interested. The military advisers – for of course they were there too – wondered whether they were about to have their suspicions

of the Chinese confirmed. The expedition made its cumber-
some way up the gorge through which the tributary ran; it
was when they reached the high valley that Voroshylov
decided he must send for Milton Cauldwell. He was pretty
sure that they had happened upon something the possibility
of which the two of them had discussed at length in a
light-hearted way one evening in Germany, in the War.

On the journey Voroshylov told Cauldwell of his suspicions. 'For some reason I wasn't particularly excited,'
Cauldwell told me, 'partly I suppose because I didn't
altogether believe him, and partly because I was quite
unprepared for the difference between these people and
ourselves. It was only when I saw the place that I began to
understand.'

It had taken them nearly a week to make their way up the
gorge. The main body of the expedition, weighed down by
equipment, had taken twice as long. Sometimes they could
walk beside the fast-moving torrent; at other times the
rocky walls of the gorge fell sheer into the water and they
would have to climb through the thick forest until they
were five or six hundred feet above the river; then they
would pass a thunderous waterfall and find themselves
beside the stream again until another wall of rock forced
them to diverge. Eventually the ground became less steep
and the forest growth began to thin out; for the first time for
days it was possible to see some way ahead. They came out
onto relatively flat land, a broad valley between two slopes
of the foothills of the Great Kinghan. This range itself rose
impressively some twenty miles ahead of them, its huge
peaks disappearing into distant Mongolia.

The first shock had been the lake.

'No one had realised how much water there was,' Cauldwell said. 'You could see the deep clefts in the rockface even
from where we were. Three or four big watercourses
coming down from the heights. At the foot of the rockface
they widened out and joined into a damned great lake. No

one had expected to find a lake there. No one had been up there. At least no one who'd been interested in making maps. There was a vast area of thickly-forested mountain country between this place and the valley of the Amur thousands of feet below. Days and days of climbing without a path and without any idea that what you were climbing towards would be worth reaching. It's a thinly populated part of the world; maybe no one had ever bothered to make the journey.'

The lake had affected the climate; this broad valley was appreciably milder than the surrounding country. The rainfall in the eastern areas of Russia is generally low, but here the waters of the lake were being used for irrigation; that was the second shock. The third was the settlement.

When I go back to Tuscany I shall ask Cauldwell to try and draw it; even if he's no artist it might help me to get an idea of the place. His description was not good. He insisted that it was a city, no other word would do. It was beautiful, but quite different from anything he had ever seen.

'The buildings had proportions I think of as classical, but if I use that word it summons up quite the wrong picture. You've got to forget any city you've ever seen. Let's say it was the opposite of primitive; you felt it was something highly civilized, evolved, and at the same time the style was human, harmonious. Hell, I don't know. How do you describe something to someone who's never seen anything like it?'

The streets were not straight, he said, and there were no squares; everything was curves and circles and crescents. There were open spaces, but they were all framed and linked by this intricate network of buildings and covered ways.

'If you think of the street map of the average American town as being a grid pattern, then this place would have to be a piece of Persian wrought iron work, or something done with tiles in the Alhambra.'

There was colour, it seems, and gold – they had gold mines up there – but nothing vulgar, nothing showy, he assured me, as if he were afraid of conjuring up some sort of Siberian Las Vegas in my mind. The colour and the gold were on the buildings, used in an apparently endless variety of complicated decorative patterns; he had not had time to discover whether any of these had special significance.

I tried to imagine it, this all but inaccessible city which was like nothing I had ever seen, built on the shores of a high mountain lake, adorned (but not vulgarly) with gold, and with colours more subtle and varied than any of ours, a city in which tall people walked or rode on mountain ponies, people with shining eyes and four fingers on each hand, descended not from our own old mother ape, Lucy or whatever it is the palaeontologists have decided to call their latest discovery, but from some other hominid, some cousin of our great-grandmother's, some offspring, Cauldwell said, even producing genealogical trees to show what he meant, some offspring of homo erectus, the ape who stood on his hind legs and yet was not a man, some other offspring of this homo erectus, some other ape – it was all too impossible, too Scobie-esque, it simply made me laugh.

Cauldwell became quite passionate.

'Why should I invent all this? You're blinkered by your own preconceptions, can't you see that? You, of all people, who must have speculated about these things, otherwise why should you have written of them? For God's sake, why should I sit here telling you stories? What would be the point of that?'

I apologized. I listened in silence. They had approached, he said, had seen the encampment on the other side of the lake where the Russian scientific expedition had set itself up, had walked between the lines of tents and come to the biological department. They were testing the lake water; they thought there might be something about it which would explain those fingers.

There was as yet no one among all these scientists who suspected what Voroshylov suspected, that these people were not properly speaking human beings at all, or at least that they were human but of a different species from our own. This was more than the scientific mind could encompass. They made observations; they were not yet prepared to make deductions.

Voroshylov took Cauldwell into the city that first evening. The streets were quiet and such of the inhabitants as they saw greeted them politely in Russian, but looked at them apprehensively. They were a fine looking race, Cauldwell said, fair, grey-eyed, tall but slim – they looked distinctly more fragile than the ordinary people of those parts.

'They seem nervous of us,' Voroshylov said. 'And we are not quite sure why. They say they have seen people like us before but not here. We have still a great deal to find out.'

'They speak Russian then?'

'Perfectly. But they don't speak it among themselves. They have another language. Or rather, several languages.'

He stopped a man who was walking towards them, the usual tall fair person with delicate features and a vivid enquiring gaze. ('A face rather like Shelley's,' Cauldwell said. 'But with a higher forehead – and of course they were all over six foot tall.')

'I wonder if you would be kind enough to speak a sentence or two of your language to my friend.' Cauldwell was impressed by the respect with which Voroshylov spoke to the stranger, a respect which he was soon to notice did not seem to be shared by the other scientists.

The Stranger spoke. (Unable to classify these people and yet aware of the inappropriate impression given by the use of the word 'tribesmen' the scientists had taken to referring to them as 'the Strangers'). The language in which he spoke seemed to have little in common with any other language –

73

it seemed like Russian without consonants, Cauldwell said, the vowel sounds running into each other without interruption. He was startled into speaking in English.

'I can't imagine what the root of that would be,' he said.

'Its only similarity to your language would be in its deep structure,' the Stranger answered politely in English. 'Being biologically innate, like yours, it's not all that dissimilar in its grammar.'

'You speak English.'

'We don't find languages very difficult. We are lucky in that respect.'

'You have more than one language of your own, my friend was telling me.'

'Yes but we use one of them more than the others. That's the one that mirrors the structure of the world of objects as you perceive them. The others are for talking about what you would call electronics, or physics, or mathematics, or music – they are the abstract languages. We can use any of the languages for poetry, or for song.'

'I suppose we couldn't sit down somewhere and talk, just for a short time – I mean, if you're not busy.'

The Stranger looked embarrassed. 'I'm sorry. This visit of yours is something we haven't been looking forward to. There are certain difficulties. We think it better if we don't answer any more questions. We have given you a lot of information. We are hoping that it will be enough and that you will now go and leave us in peace.'

'My friend has only just arrived,' Voroshylov interposed. 'I hadn't told him about your feelings. The rest of the expedition knows them of course.'

The Stranger again expressed his regrets. Before they parted he rather hesitantly asked Cauldwell his name. 'Perhaps, if it seemed – necessary – I could get in touch with you.'

Voroshylov and Cauldwell walked on through the city. This was a cold climate and the City was not one where life was lived on the streets, but they saw enough to sustain Cauldwell's already high level of admiration and astonishment. It seemed very quiet. The Strangers they passed returned their greetings, but then turned away. They came to a central space with a long two-storeyed building, serpentine in shape and much decorated, beside it. Here numbers of people were dancing, or not dancing exactly but moving as if to music – but there was no music. As they passed beneath some low trees which grew to one side of the square, they seemed to direct their steps in such a way as to allow certain leafy branches to touch their foreheads, always in the same place. Some of the Strangers were circulating in this way by themselves but others went in twos or threes, talking, and from time to time greeting other Strangers or asking yet others, who were newly arrived, to join them as they moved.

'I think they can induce a light trance in this way,' Voroshylov said. 'But it seems to be a social event; it happens in the early evening. Look, this is the building we think is their temple.'

In the temple, there was movement and light, some chanting, some gold. 'But what God?' I asked.

'They were always so polite,' said Cauldwell. 'So keen to show they were really much the same as us. It was their way of propitiating us. They were always trying to reassure us. They told us our language was much the same, though to us it seemed totally different. In the same way they said oh yes they had a religion, a God; their whole function was religious, they told us, they were the expression of the joy of the creative mind; only they had a different concept of God, it was in no sense an anthropomorphic one. When Hal used to talk about it he said, "We are God's dream, we are the symbols which crowd the dreaming mind of the Creator." I wrote that down. I was rather pleased with it. He was pleased with it too. He was pleased with it because he had used our kind of religious language – but what did our understanding of it correspond to in his mind? About a hundredth part of what its meaning was to him. That was always the trouble, all the time.'

'But they had priests?'

'They had priestly functions, but they were performed by different people at different times. These functions were complicated, like all their ceremonies, highly ritualized and apparently unchanging; to that extent I suppose it didn't matter who performed them. Perhaps everyone had their turn, I never found out. I did discover that performances were criticized keenly and good performances were much appreciated. This was true of all the expressions of their communal life; they had a great love of ceremonial, drama, theatre, every occasion of that kind. But there was so much we didn't find out – so many stupid questions we asked and so many important ones we failed to ask – and we had so little time.'

As I say, I had to piece it all together. He told me what he knew of those people, and of their past history, and of what became of them, all in a jumble of recollections and comments and inconsequences. I made what sense I could of it afterwards; though I too asked stupid questions and forgot the most important ones.

*

The first thing was, they knew all about us. They had been keeping written records while our own ancestors were still learning how to sharpen a flint. Their first encounters with our species had been with prehistoric man as he emerged in China; they recognized him as dangerous and kept out of his way. They had been keeping out of our way ever since. There had once been more of them; ruined cities remain in other of those remote valleys. They fought a war once, with the Scythians, in the third century BC. Herodotus mentions an encounter which seems likely to have been this distant battle. They were totally defeated and many of them were killed. They retreated to the remotest of their valleys, and recognized that Homo Sapiens was their superior in physical strength and command of weaponry. They watched our development, their explorers moved among the populations of the world without being detected, but they never again entered into conflict with us. They lived in secret, believing that if we discovered them we would destroy them.

'You are hunters,' Hal said to Cauldwell. 'Also it is your instinct to destroy what you don't understand.'

They had looked instead, he said, to other parts of the Universe.

'This is the bit I could kick myself for not having asked more about,' Cauldwell told me. 'There was so much to find out and my first concern was to discover how they worked, their actual physical make-up – the more one found out the more different they turned out to be, far more different than they appeared at first sight. The difficulty was that their perceptions were in many ways different from ours and that meant that their view of the world and their way of explaining it was different. They could use our language but we couldn't use theirs, so a lot of what they tried to convey to us was really not communicable. One great difference in brain function seemed to be that they could deal very much more easily than we can with concepts detached from sensory perception. The sort of advanced physics which our scientists are only just beginning to understand and which most human beings find quite beyond their mental grasp seemed elementary to them. They seemed capable of perceiving things more or less as we perceive them and at the same time of perceiving them – literally seeing them – as Einstein calculated that they must be by the use of mathematics. This gave them a different view of the universe – they didn't feel lost in it, as we tend to feel since the discoveries of physics; they felt, as in a different way perhaps we felt long ago when we were more ignorant and more superstitious, a close personal association with the whole of creation.'

'But they could travel through space?'

'I think so. But we never found out for sure. There were some big hangars on the outskirts of the city which they never allowed us into. If they had some form of space ship it could have been there. I couldn't really follow what Hal said about all that. For one thing, their concept of time was quite different from ours – or rather, as with their way of seeing things, they seemed to be able to be both inside our sort of time-scale and outside any sort of time at all – all at the same time. It made it extraordinarily difficult to know what they really meant when they spoke. Certainly their eyes were such that they could see stars we can't see, but when Hal spoke of life on these stars, I wasn't sure whether he meant that his people had colonized them or that they had visited them and found other beings there already, or whether he was trying to put into our language some non-perceptual concept which was quite beyond me. Whenever he wanted to explain something, he put it into human terms because that was the only way in which we could understand it, our species being self-centred and earthbound in a way that theirs was not; so that I came to believe that some of the things he told us were not factually and literally true so much as parables; but I was never quite sure about this. Certainly, if there are any more of them, they are on other stars.'

★

The Strangers had decided among themselves that their best policy was one of polite reserve. They had always known that one day some inquisitive members of the Homo Sapiens species might reach their city and they knew that such an event would be a serious threat to their survival. They felt their best hope was to persuade the visitors that they were members of the same species, living peace-

78

fully, constituting no danger to Mankind and desiring only to be left alone. The day after Cauldwell's arrival, three Strangers appeared at the camp and asked to speak to the leader of the expedition. When they were led before Dr Nevtushenko in his tent, they politely besought him to move his expedition on. They said that they had answered all the many questions they had been asked to the best of their ability, that they had nothing more to impart, and that they would be grateful now to be left in peace. Dr Nevtushenko promised to respect their privacy but said that his expedition would like to stay a little longer.

'Please go on with your normal lives,' he said. 'We won't interfere with you in any way, but we should like to make a few more observations and prepare a report. After all,' he added, 'you will be in the newspapers.'

Telling me this, Cauldwell said, 'This was a highly educated Russian, remember, a trained scientist who had risen to the top of his profession. It was beyond the power of his imagination to conceive of a people who would not willingly sacrifice their privacy and peace of mind for the sake of having their name in the newspapers – and they say that it is only in the West that scientists have been corrupted by the media. Anyway, we stayed. I was as keen as anyone. I wanted to know about these people. I wanted to know every damned thing about them. I had to possess that information, in a way to possess the people themselves if you like, to make them mine. I had to do it.'

The Strangers, seeming always quieter and quieter, went about what seemed to be their daily lives. They gave the expedition bread and vegetables and gold filigree ornaments; they gave them vaguer and vaguer replies to the questions they were asked.

'It is the same,' they kept saying. 'We are the same.'

The same marriage customs, the same games, the same food, the same system of exchange – well, they used barter instead of money, but it came to the same thing – sex, divorce, oh yes of course, children, yes, brought up in the same way, birth control, yes, death ceremonies, crime, systems of justice, property, yes, yes, all the same. In reality, Cauldwell came to believe, almost nothing was the same.

'There was quite a lot that looked the same. Property for instance. Certainly there was personal property; but when you went into it a little deeper it turned out as so often, that words meant different things – their word for "mine" meant something to do with spheres of responsibility but it didn't quite seem to mean "not yours", any more than "yours" seemed quite to mean "not mine". The thing was, they were desperate to get rid of us. They were convinced that the best way of doing so was to make themselves as uninteresting as possible. Poor things, they failed. It was beyond even their powers to make themselves uninteresting.'

By this time, the photograph which I had seen in the newspaper cutting which had fallen out of the paperback copy of *Scobie and the Other Ape* in Cauldwell's house in Tuscany had been sent back to Moscow and had appeared in a daily newspaper. 'Descendants of Russian settlers discovered in remote Siberian valley. A team of scientists on an expedition in South Eastern Siberia have come upon a settlement long isolated from the outside world, which they believe to be descended from eighth century Russian traders . . .'' They had to be Russian; anything else would have been politically undesirable. By now the biologists, having discovered nothing peculiar in the water or the soil, were trying to persuade pregnant women to leave the valley and come with them to the nearest hospital to be x-rayed; the geologists were talking of opening up the gold-mines, the engineers of building a road.

One evening, the scientists in their camp heard a series of explosions, and went out to look towards the city of the Strangers. The sky above the centre of the city was full of multi-coloured stars. There were more explosions, more showers of stars; it was a few minutes before the scientists realised that the Strangers were not declaring war, or escaping in space rockets to other planets; they were letting off fireworks. Because of the increasing nervousness with which it was clear that the Strangers regarded the scientists, it had been decided that none of the latter should go into the city in the evening, but should leave its inhabitants in peace after dark; on this occasion, their curiosity overcame them and most of them walked quietly through the deserted streets towards the central square. It looked as if the entire population of the city must be there, a crowd of men, women and children, making, as they watched the fire-works, more or less the same sounds as their Homo Sapiens cousins on similar occasions, 'Oooh' when the rockets went up, 'Aaah' when they exploded. Cauldwell said he had never seen fireworks that went so far so fast or produced more astonishing bursts of colour and light. At first, there was tremendous banging – at the same time loud music was playing – he could not see where it was coming from but though the harmonies were unfamiliar the insistent rhythm was much like that of our own popular music. Some of the strangers were dancing, others clapping their hands or singing, but as the display of fireworks became more and more dazzling, they fell silent. The music stopped, the explosions stopped, only the extraordinarily intricate pat-terns of lights appeared and reappeared in a continuously renewed and endlessly elaborate spectacle. So absorbing was it that Cauldwell told me it was some time before he noticed the silence. When he looked at the faces of the Stran-gers, they appeared to be in some kind of ecstasy.

'It was an extraordinarily intense experience. Even I felt it. What they were feeling I can only guess, since their capacity for every kind of sensation was greater than ours. As the display began gradually to simplify, gradually to slow down, so the people began to sing, in the multiple vowel sounds which were their language. It was as if they

81

woke from their trance singing. The fireworks continued, but more slowly, the rockets went up with the sort of noise our own rockets make, we came, as it were, down to earth, while they sang. When I looked at their faces, I felt for the first time like an intruder – I hadn't felt it before – no doubt I should have done, but I didn't. I assumed as a matter of course that it was our right to expose everything that we could find out about these people to the rest of the world – yes, and to become rich and famous by doing so, though that wasn't my first consideration – and I'd hardly given a thought to what might become of them. In so far as I had given it a thought, I didn't care – it was a totally secondary consideration. But now as I looked at their singing faces I felt moved, I felt for the first time really quite violently sympathetic towards them. It was at that moment that I saw the Stranger I had talked to on the first evening. We smiled, lifted our hands. Not far away from me, one of the photographers in our group took a photograph with a flash. The Strangers nearest him immediately put their hands to their heads and moved away. He took another and they began to run, still holding their heads. He called out reassuringly that he had finished, and pointed his camera at another group. This group reacted in the same way, holding their heads and moving away. We had noticed before that they disliked being photographed – indeed they had asked us not to do it and we had begun to use our cameras much less – but this reaction was unusually strong. The photographer put his camera away making conciliatory signs but that part of the crowd which was near enough to know of the incident was clearly upset. We thought we'd better go. Anyway the party was over.'

*

It was the next day that the Stranger who had smiled at Cauldwell came to see him in the tent which he shared with Voroshylov. He told them his name; the nearest an American could get to it was 'Hal'. Hal had come to beg them to leave. He told them what they already knew. 'It's something we have been trying to conceal from you. We are not Homo Sapiens. We are a differently species, and because we are differently made, what you are doing to us is destroying us. This morning one of the women who was photographed last night died.'

He explained that their brains were differently constituted in almost every way and that the chemicals in their brain fluid were particularly sensitive to any kind of electronic or electrical interference or any manipulation of sound waves or light rays. The mere fact that the scientists had radio equipment in their camp had been enough to give the entire population of the city severe headaches. Because they felt that their survival depended on their concealing their origin they had not been able to prevent the scientists from unwittingly inflicting on them any number of tortures.

'If we can't persuade you to leave us alone, you will destroy us. The woman who died this morning died mad. This is why we are the unsuccessful species and you are the evolutionary success. Our brains are so highly developed that we need far fewer tools than you. We also achieve far higher levels of consciousness. But on Earth we have one enemy with whom we cannot compete, you. It's not just that you're more aggressive, it's that our brains are instruments of such delicacy that you with your machines, your instruments, your crude intellectual probing, if I may put it like that, can't help but destroy them, even when you don't mean to. If you should ever mean to, all you would have to do would be to surround us with ordinary portable radios, tuned to any programme you like, and within twenty-four hours, we should be destroyed. The molecules in the brain cells which set off the passage of messages between nerves by releasing substances rather like neurotransmitters you have in your own brains but more chemically complicated, are fatally interfered with by the radio-frequency energy which escapes into the air whenever you are using any kind of radio equipment. It causes a sort of mental chaos. You can imagine the results. That's just one of the disasters you can precipitate. The fact is that in spite of any superiorities you may think we have as a species, we have this one fatal vulnerability. Our brains are as much more advanced than yours as yours are than the chimpanzee's, but they are highly delicate as a result. It makes us an evolutionary mistake as far as the Earth is concerned—that is, as long as you're here. You may wipe yourselves out, being the species above all species which goes in for internecine strife. We could probably colonize the Earth after that.'

Cauldwell asked for more information about their brains. What was it exactly, he said, that happened to them when they were exposed to Homo Sapiens. Hal told him it was more or less as though a fuse blew.

'Or think how even among yourselves you torture each other by inflicting mental pain. Imagine that doubled and redoubled. You call it "getting on people's nerves". It's nervous pressure, the "stringing up" of the nervous system by constant exposure to an infinitely less delicate one. After the headaches come digestive troubles. Half the population of our city can't eat now. Then there's nervous exhaustion, sometimes even an explosion of violence, unheard of among our people under normal conditions. Even the weight of the personality of one of you in the same room is a powerful threat to our mental equilibrium. For us you are a *powerful* species – stupid, cruel and above all powerful. I hope I haven't hurt your feelings.'

Cauldwell, being American, said no. I would have said yes, if only to show that the Strangers hadn't a monopoly of delicate feelings; but Americans tend to think it a mark of sincerity to acquiesce in the denigration of the human species; it's probably a sort of guilt because they know

84

they're in fact the only nation left which still believes in all those nineteenth century notions like Progress and the Perfectibility of Man. Anyway he said no, he wasn't offended. Hal, not quite convinced, assured him that the Strangers much admired our vitality, our curiosity, our art; he then repeated his plea to be left alone.

Cauldwell and Voroshylov asked him to leave and return in a few hours' time; they promised they would have decided by then how best to help him. Voroshylov was all for going straight to Moscow, putting on pressure 'at the highest level' and getting the expedition recalled. He said he had the ear of the Government Minister responsible and would be able to persuade him that it was a waste of money for the expedition to linger where they were – they were being diverted from their proper concerns. It was all something to do with the inner mysteries of the Russian hierarchy and if Voroshylov said he could do it, Cauldwell tended to believe him; no news of the expedition had penetrated beyond the confines of Russia. Voroshylov said he had been moved to tears at the previous night's firework ceremony. (The Strangers had decided to put it on, Hal had told them, in spite of the danger of attracting too much attention from the scientists, because their people were, as he put it, 'so much in need of solace'.)

'How could we have it on our conscience to have destroyed a whole species?' said Voroshylov. 'And a species such as that. A species more closely related to our own than any other.'

Cauldwell was less emotional about it. He thought there was no need to rush.

'I was damned if I was going to give in without a fight,' he told me. 'No one else knew who these people were. The others were certainly puzzled, but they were going to need many more tests and observations before they were likely to get around to the right hypothesis. It was more than I could stand to say goodbye to the whole thing, call off the expedition and never see these creatures again. I thought we ought to strike a bargain.'

In the end, they agreed on a proposition which they put to Hal when he came back later the same day. They said that they would arrange for the expedition to be called off if he himself would come with them to Moscow, telling them on the journey and while they were in Moscow all he could about his people and submitting to certain tests and examinations in a Moscow hospital while the necessary negotiations to call off the expedition were made by Voroshylov. They promised not to keep him in Moscow longer than Voroshylov needed to complete his negotiations, and they promised also that the greatest care would be taken of Hal himself now that they were aware of the dangers, and now that he himself was able to speak freely of them. They promised also not to make public the information he gave them except in such a way as to make absolutely certain of his own and his species' inviolability. (Cauldwell told me that what he had in mind was to publish the whole thing as a piece of theoretical speculation, in America, where no one would be likely to trace the theory to its origin.) Hal agreed.

★

Hal was not particularly interested in Moscow; he had been there before. He had spent several days sight-seeing ten years earlier, keeping his hands in his pockets. He preferred to sit in Voroshylov's comfortable flat, listening to Beethoven Quartets.

'It was maddening,' said Cauldwell. 'He had the thing turned so quiet you could only just hear it. Opus 135 like a thin little insect just above silence.'

Voroshylov was highly thought of in Moscow at that time – he had taken the approved line about the Lysenko case and seemed to Cauldwell to be on the point of becoming a hero of the Revolution. Cauldwell was rather impressed, especially as he thought he was quite wrong about Lysenko; he admired his political acumen, knowing it was something he would never have himself. The three of them stayed in Voroshylov's flat and were looked after by his maid. 'Imagine!' said Cauldwell. 'A maid in Moscow.'

When Hal wasn't listening to Beethoven, he talked. Cauldwell asked questions and took notes; Voroshylov presumably walked the corridors of power. On the third day, Hal insisted that they should leave.

Cauldwell begged him to stay even one more day so that they could complete the series of tests Voroshylov had arranged at a Moscow hospital, he even tried to persuade Voroshylov to say that he needed more time to arrange for the calling off of the expedition, but the fact was that Voroshylov was more anxious to protect the Strangers than Cauldwell was; he had got the necessary instructions from the Minister and was not going to pretend he hadn't. Hal said it was very important that they should go. Still asking questions, Cauldwell acquiesced. On the journey Hal became increasingly distressed.

In Moscow, he had been fairly light-hearted, in spite of his anxiety for his people. He liked caviare and Russian jokes; he and Voroshylov had talked about Russian literature when Cauldwell was impatient to get on with his inquisition: they had gone on for hours about how the Strangers' literature was much the same, only that their fancy was freer and their understanding of the use of fiction as a language like the language of music was more complicated. Cauldwell had found all this too vague; he wanted to know about genetic codes and haemoglobin genes. He was bored when Voroshylov drank vodka and gave Hal a demonstration of Russian dancing, and irritated when Hal claimed to enjoy it immensely.

'I was right too,' he said. 'It *was* a waste of time.' On the long train journey from Moscow to Irkutsk, Hal became less and less talkative. In answer to their queries, he said he was not feeling well. Finally he said he was anxious, he was afraid that things were going badly in his valley. They tried to reassure him but he said he knew, his head was full of disharmony. The closer they came the more desperate he grew. To satisfy him, they travelled on without pause, and took the pony track up the gorge in a fairly exhausted state. Hal had become deathly pale and could only moan faintly when they spoke to him. He refused food and drink and communicated such a sense of frantic concern that they pushed on as fast as the ponies could go. They completed the journey up the gorge in less than a week.

It was night by the time they reached the valley, and very cold. There was a full moon, but over the city there was a light that was not moonlight. Hal pushed his tired pony into a trot; the others followed. When he came near to the city and saw that it was nothing but a smouldering ruin, he jumped off his pony and began to run towards it; then he held out his arms and sank to his knees. When they caught up with him he was in the same position, his head thrown back; the orange glow from the burnt city was stronger than the white light of the moon and illuminated his expression of extreme anguish. As they waited, appalled, and uncertain of how to help him, he gave two or three violent jerks of his whole body and fell on his face, apparently unconscious.

*

What had happened was exactly what Hall had said would happen; unfortunately he had failed to realize how imminent the catastrophe was. Dr Nevtushenko, who was in charge of the expedition, had been increasingly uneasy after Cauldwell, Voroshylov and Hal had left for Moscow. His brief was to investigate that part of Siberia in order to suggest what, if anything, could be done to develop the potentialities of the area. The discovery of a curious and apparently unclassifiable settlement of people living where it was thought no one lived constituted a diversion; it was something that ought really to be reported back and poss-ibly made the object of another quite different expedition. The trouble was that the people seemed to be so odd in every way that it was hard to know what to put in even that brief preliminary report. However, winter was on the way, money as well as time was beginning to run out. Dr Nevtushenko decided to spend one more day filming, so as to have a record with which to whet the appetites of the relevant experts and authorities in Moscow, and then to return down the gorge. He told the Strangers of his inten-tion, they begged him not to move in the cameras, he told them it was for one day only and that that would be the end of it, he told them as politely as he could that he could see no sense in their objection, and he over-ruled it. The cameras moved in using flashes where necessary. The camera crew used walkie-talkies to co-ordinate their filming. By the end of the day there was madness in the streets.

Hal had explained that violence of any kind was very rare among the Strangers. He said he did not know why this was but thought it might have been to some extent culturally induced after their disastrous war against the Scythians.

'It's not only that we are not such an aggressive species as you are, it's rather that violence is taboo – just as incest is for you. In other words, it does go on, but very little, and it is considered quite shocking.' (Cauldwell regretted not having asked him then whether incest was also taboo for them.) 'Young men are known occasionally to join together to form boxing clubs although it is much disapproved of, but even that is highly formalized like all our athletic sports. So the idea of a quarrel ending in a fight is really quite inconceivable.'

So when, under the intense pressure to which they were submitted by the day's filming and which their desire to keep their difference a secret prevented them from explain-ing to Dr Nevtushenko, they began, as the woman who had died earlier had done, to go out of their minds, the fury which overtook them was not even then directed outside themselves. They did not attack the photographers or break the cameras. They did not attack each other. They went, in response to some crazed mis-direction of their instincts, to their firework store.

Music and fireworks were their best loved and understood diversions; in both they had reached such a pitch of perfection as to be able to induce in themselves a high state of ecstasy; in its most intense manifestation, they listened to silent music and watched silent fireworks. Whether there was also something religious in their attitude to fire, Cauldwell was not certain, but some of their religious ceremonies were attended by fireworks. Having invented gunpowder before the Chinese, they had used it exclusively for making fireworks, but it seems likely that they were also using other materials; the extraordinary exhibition the scientists had seen was far beyond anything that could be produced by the means familiar to us.

The supplies were kept in a large building near the central square. The maddened crowd rushed it, and began to explode the fireworks, whether in the hope that the customary display could relieve their mental agony or in response to some obscurer urge towards self-destruction, no one knows. In their frenzy they mishandled the things; the store caught fire. There were tremendous explosions; the demented Strangers seized the rockets and threw them at other buildings. Soon the whole city was in flames. The camera men ran to safety but the Strangers did not follow them. When the supply of fireworks to throw on to the already burning buildings ran out, they threw themselves. Such was their frenzy, they hurled themselves at the flames and burned to death. Not one of them survived.

*

Cauldwell and Voroshylov did not know the full story of the disaster until later, but they were both possessed by the feeling that not only must they try to save Hal's life, they must conceal him. They could see figures moving around the ruined city, dark against the redness of the still smouldering buildings; from time to time tongues of flame rose briefly into the air as the fire discovered something still unconsumed. The scientists, now that the heat was less intense, were looking for survivors, discovering the extent of the disaster; none of them was looking towards his own camp. Wrapping Hal's big cloak around him, Cauldwell and Voroshylov supported him between them and carried him unobserved into their tent, where they set about trying to revive him. He appeared to be in a coma, but was breathing peacefully; his heart seemed to be beating normally. Cauldwell left Voroshylov tenderly sponging his forehead and his long pale four-fingered hands, and went to find out what had happened. The shocked spectators round the edges of the burnt city told him what they had seen, and that it seemed unlikely that any of the Strangers had survived. He went back to his tent with the news that the unconscious Hal seemed to be the last of his species.

Voroshylov was weeping – 'You know what Russians are,' said Cauldwell – and his one thought was to save Hal. 'They will destroy him as they destroyed the others,' he kept saying.

'I couldn't help agreeing with him,' said Cauldwell. 'How could those bastards have been to damned stupid? We all knew these people weren't savages – if they said they didn't want to be photographed, they must have had some reason for it. If anything I was even angrier than Voroshylov because I was also guilty. I hadn't seen the urgency. Voroshylov had been willing to let the whole thing go, to save those people. I hadn't, I'd wanted something out of them first. Voroshylov could have had a clearer conscience than I had. Not that he was thinking along those lines. He was thinking only of how to save Hal, and at the same time grieving, and reproaching himself. He was a generous-hearted man, and a good scientist. Anyway, as you see, we got Hal out.'

He had come out of his coma after a few days. The expedition was packing up all round them – there had been arguments and recriminations, the mood was bad – no one had noticed that Cauldwell and Voroshylov were keeping their tent closed to all-comers. As soon as they thought it safe to move him, they bundled him onto a pony and Cauldwell took him down the gorge. Voroshylov stayed behind – officially he was still attached to the expedition and had to play his part in moving it on – but he told them to go to his flat in Moscow and wait for him there. Hal had still not spoken, but he seemed to be able to move all his limbs, though with difficulty. The expression on his face was calm, Cauldwell said, but extraordinarily dimmed. When they brought him food, he took it with a smile which was like an echo of the smile they had become used to. After a difficult journey Cauldwell got him to bed in Voroshylov's flat and began to try to nurse him back to health.

He gave him light meals and what he could of physio-therapy. He played him Beethoven Quartets, as quietly as he had heard them before; he bought him musical scores and gave them to him to read. Very slowly, the power of speech returned, at first only in his own language, which was incomprehensible to Cauldwell, but eventually in other languages as well. By the time Voroshylov turned up in Moscow Hal was moving and speaking almost normally. It was clear that he had lost all memory not only of the disaster but of most of his life before it; it also gradually became clear that his mental powers were very much diminished. He had become like a rather simple and child-like member of the Homo Sapiens species. 'To his kind,' said Voroshylov, 'that would be the equivalent of being severely sub-normal.'

'I wasn't so sure of that,' Cauldwell said. 'The funny thing about the Strangers was that in spite of their extra-ordinary mental powers, they always were a bit child-like. I thought he might recover completely. I thought that for years. But he never has.'

Voroshylov was in a rather anxious state when he arrived in Moscow. He had quarrelled badly with Dr Nevtushenko. He had not meant to but his indignation had overcome his caution. Nevtushenko was apparently quite an important fellow and Voroshylov was in danger of losing his job.

'I shall have to behave very correctly for a bit. The best thing would be if you were to take Hal right away from Russia. Take him to America, where no one could possibly find out about any of this. No Russian scientist is ever going to let anyone in the West hear about something which ended so badly. Take him to America and I will get in touch with you as soon as I can.'

*

In the event, Cauldwell went to Italy with Hal; he had an aunt who lived in Fiesole. His own position in America was likely to be embarrassing. He had been absent for over a month from his university post, and he had failed even to write a letter of excuse. To turn up with a vague story of having been to Russia, and accompanied by someone who would have the scantiest of documentation and no entry permit – all this in America in the 'fifties – was really more or less out of the question.

Voroshylov was able to provide Hal with a false passport – such things were obtainable in Moscow if you knew the right people – and Cauldwell and Hal flew to Rome with the idea that if Cauldwell's aunt proved amenable, he would leave Hal with her for a week or two while he went to America to try to sort out the situation there. The aunt, an elderly widow whose late husband had been in the diplomatic service, was ferociously anti-Communist. It was not hard to give her the impression that Hal was a refugee from the Russian regime and therefore in her eyes a hero. She

93

took them one day for a drive in the country, to have lunch in a little restaurant she knew in the hills somewhere towards Siena. Cauldwell and Hal went for a walk afterwards while she dozed on the terrace of the restaurant in the autumn sun, wrapped in her fur coat and with her Pekingese asleep on her knee. It was then that Cauldwell first thought of coming to live there. Hal seemed happier that day than he had been since the disaster, and in Italy the question of papers could be solved so much more easily than in America; it would be a question of giving the right person in the right bureaucracy the right amount of money.

'I'd had enough of science,' he said. 'Perhaps I saw it as a sort of penance, something I owed Hal. I felt it was my fault, not exclusively mine but very largely mine. I had known the dangers, I had not acted quickly enough, partly for selfish reasons. I had taken away from him all the others of his kind; I had taken away his reason. The least I could do was spend the rest of my life looking after him.'

The aunt, delighted to have them living nearby, had helped with a loan for the house. Cauldwell's name had since become quite well known among modern composers; it was a useful source of income. An understanding of music was one of the things he and Hal shared. 'Of course he's lost what he used to have in that way,' said Cauldwell. 'But some of the harmonies I've introduced have come from him. Maybe they're echoes.'

'And Voroshylov?' I asked him.

'I wrote to him of course. I only had one reply, in the early days. He said he would try to come out, to see us, but he never came. Eventually I wrote to one of the other scientists to ask for news, and I got a letter back saying Voroshylov had not been well for some time, he had left his job, and was now, this fellow understood, a voluntary patient in a mental hospital. God knows what that meant. Maybe he wasn't so clever at the political game as I thought he was.'

We sat in silence for some moments.

'I liked the sound of Voroshylov,' I said eventually.

'He was a nice man,' said Cauldwell, looking suddenly very tired.

He had been talking for a long time, during which we had consumed a good deal more of his excellent Chianti. His eyelids were beginning to drop.

'I've kept you up for hours,' I said getting to my feet. 'I'll go at once. I couldn't let you stop, you know, it was all so extraordinary.'

'I'll drive you back.'

'No, no of course I'll walk.'

'It's dark. It won't take me a moment to run you back in the car. I'll just tell Hal what I'm doing.'

He began to go upstairs.

'Won't you wake him?'

'He doesn't sleep a great deal. He'll be awake I expect.'

I followed him upstairs, and stood behind him as he opened the door into Hal's room. It was a white-washed room with dark wooden beams on the ceiling. The small windows were shuttered against the night and the one oil lamp on the table beside which Hal was sitting in a large cushioned cane chair threw only a faint light into the further corners of the room; I dimly made out shelves of books and oriental hangings and a large brass bed; it seemed a comfortable room.

Cauldwell said he was going to drive me home. Hal, surprised at our being up so late, nevertheless gave us the benefit of his serene gaze, smiled again, said goodbye again. Cauldwell shut the door.

On the way back to my house in the car I said, 'Oughtn't he to reproduce?'

'How?'

'Well surely, some nice local girl . . .'

'Mammals don't breed across species.'

'But surely if you explained the necessity?'

'He's forgotten that he's any different. He wouldn't believe me.'

'Couldn't you make him believe you?'

'He'd think I was mad. It would upset him terribly. Besides nothing would happen, don't you see? You can't cross breed between species.'

'Or artificial insemination or something – or, look, didn't you say there might be more of them, in other parts of the universe? Oughtn't some of his sperm to be kept somewhere frozen in case one of them turns up? Surely you could persuade him to do that?'

Cauldwell changed gear with an unnecessary jerk – we were turning into the road which led to my house.

'Why should I?' he said, unexpectedly angry. 'Why the hell should I persuade him to do anything of the kind? I saw what happened last time. It would be the same. If there was another one of his kind, what would become of it? The same thing. If there was another one, they'd destroy that one too.'

He spoke with such bitterness that I didn't answer. We arrived at my house.

'For Christ's sake—' he began, still angry.

'I know, I know. I shan't say a word, I promise you that. But I'd like to come and see you again some time, that's all.'

'Fine,' he said, but I could tell that he was still not reassured.

*

I thought I would leave him in peace for a day or two; I didn't want to be importunate. But on the second day, I was woken by the peremptory sound of a scooter's horn. I went out in my dressing gown to find the postman sitting on his Vespa holding out a telegram from Phil Pope.

'Likeliest can sell Scobie USTV series. Principal in London four days. Come at once discuss.'

I telephoned from the bar in the village.

'It's not very convenient, Phil. Surely you can make a contract – you don't need me.'

'He wants you to do the script. He has to meet you. This could be the big break.'

I went back to London.

It wasn't the big break; I knew the moment I saw the American that I couldn't work with him. He talked extensively about his plans for the series all the same, and said he would call me before he left the next day. I never heard from him again. A few days later, Phil had a letter from him saying he was not interested in pursuing the scheme any further. Phil said it was my fault that his enthusiasm cooled, but I never thought for a moment that he had the financial backing; it was all talk. Agents are gullible creatures.

So now it is August. I haven't finished the book I went to Italy to write. I can't afford the fare to go back, quite apart from the fact that I usually find it too hot there in August. I am trying to finish the book, so as to raise a bit of money. In the meantime, of course, I think about Cauldwell's story.

No one apart from Phil Pope knows that I am back from Italy – I told Bettina I should probably be there until September. The telephone doesn't ring. I try to think about Scobie, and the ghastly Eileen and the secretive Rameses, but I don't, I think about Cauldwell and Hal, and Voroshylov, and the high valley of the tributary of the upper Amur.

When you are alone for a long time, your mind takes strange courses. If you have been concentrating on a particular set of ideas, your mind, to relieve pressure, might begin to play with those ideas, submit them to some other logic, the logic of dream; you might start to fantasize. I have never to my knowledge done such a thing before but the possibility does exist that I may have imagined it all, or dreamt it, or half-imagined it. Alternatively, Cauldwell may have been fantasizing. Or he might have made the whole thing up, to amuse himself, to see if he could convince me; he may have gone back to Hal in fits of laughter. 'He really believed me. He said you ought to provide a sperm bank.' But I don't think so somehow. And if it's all true, I feel a kind of responsibility about it.

Voroshylov is lost, in a Soviet lunatic asylum. Cauldwell is deeply embittered. Of course, I hate the human race too – naturally, we're a perfectly frightful species, you've only to read a newspaper to see that, and yet – ought we not to know about these cousins of ours?

I accept what Cauldwell says about reproduction, but he surely couldn't object to my seeing the detailed notes about the Strangers which he made during those three days in Moscow with Hal, or to my questioning him as to anything he can remember about the way of life of these people.

A long time ago I went to school in the North of England, where I was born. The school has been abolished now, as a punishment for being elitist, which is funny in a way when you think how hard I tried to disown it after it had got me into Oxford because I thought it wasn't elitist enough. At the time I was there it was just School to me and I had nothing particular against it; I passed through it peacefully enough, taking what I wanted, forgetting the rest. They taught us Christianity and I forgot nearly all of that; but at some time or other someone told us about the idea of redemption – not atonement, that I never understood, but redemption – and I have a vague picture at the back of my mind of dust dancing in the several shafts of sunlight which came through the not very attractive nineteenth century stained glass of the School Chapel windows – just dancing dust and the idea of redemption.

It seems that these Strangers were in some ways better than we are. They were our cousins. If we knew every detail that Cauldwell could tell me about them, not the things that interested him so much, not the genetic codes and the haemoglobin genes, but the way they organized themselves, how they solved their conflicts, maintained order, educated their young, their heirarchies and categories, rights and duties, economics, culture, rituals, if we knew all that – or as much of it as Cauldwell could tell me – we could learn from it, we could redeem ourselves.

I shall have to go back to Italy. It's not really because I can't afford the fare that I haven't gone already, it's because I am reluctant to go in case I walk the way I went and turn down the path towards the house and find nothing there, no house, no crowding flower pots, no neat wood pile, no spotted dog, or in case I find the house but Cauldwell and Hal are not as I remember them, in case it is proved to have been a delusion, or a joke, or a dream, or a mistake; but I shall have to go. If we knew we once had had such cousins, who knows what we might do?

A Glimpse of Sion's Glory

'Do they bring you breakfast in bed, the perfectly trained Embassy staff? Or do you sit downstairs at a highly polished table, drinking your coffee while Robert taps his boiled egg and sighs for English bacon? Whatever you do it with be de rigueur. Here is a letter which is not at all de rigueur. Slip it under your napkin perhaps, wait until Robert is safely at his desk, hedged about by diligent young men who have been up for hours underlining passages in the newspapers for his attention. Please read it slowly, dear Alison. It is my True Confession.'

'I hope that long letter's not from my mother,' said Robert.

'It's from Raymond. He says it's his true confession.'

'Good. I'll read it this evening. I'll look forward to that.' He dabbed his mouth with his napkin, rose briskly to his feet. 'I'm off. See you this evening. It's the commercial lunch today.'

Alison folded the letter, and went downstairs to speak to Fiona, the social secretary. Alison's daughters, Charlotte and Amy, laughed at Fiona, for being so conventional, such a Sloane Ranger, they said. Alison herself was not quite certain where the dividing line between categories lay; Charlotte and Amy, beautiful calm schoolgirls before whose ordered intellects examiners capitulated without a fight, seemed to her not stylistically very different from Fiona. Obviously they were more intelligent. Charlotte had not yet taken A levels but had already made provisional arrangements with the Oxford College of her choice; no one pretended there was any question of her failing the examination. Amy preferred Cambridge; she said Oxford people seemed so frivolous; she was fifteen. They were not prigs, just astonishingly competent; Robert had been like that.

Fiona was quite competent too, though only about severely practical things like cars and telephones and arrangements. She was like girls Alison had known when she was eighteen in the 'fifties, a type that in the intervening years seemed to have disappeared but in fact had merely gone underground, to re-emerge in a more favourable social climate, headscarf and string of pearls in place, ringing nasal tones as confident as ever. The years of eclipse had only added a certain steeliness. The girls Alison remembered seemed gentle creatures in comparison with Fiona. Fiona had attack. Fiona could say, 'Everyone loves the way you make Embassy life so informal,' or 'I thought you wouldn't be needing the car so I said I'd drop in and see some chums on the way back from the airport,' or 'Are the Tompkins coming? How super. They knew my father in Hong Kong,' so that these apparently harmless remarks could seem as irritating as a sleepy fly on a bare arm. Alison, thought of by her friends as gentle to a fault, nourished a considerable dislike for Fiona. As she went downstairs she thought how pleasant it would have been to have been able to expose her to Raymond, who would undoubtedly have shaken her, and possibly shocked her, but Raymond never seemed to come and stay with them these days, was immured, she supposed, in his little room in All Souls producing the long-delayed great work on number, whatever that meant. It was to be called A Glimpse of Sion's Glory, that he had told her when she had last seen him, at a party in England in the summer in someone's garden. A Glimpse of Sion's Glory, he had said. If anyone had had such a glimpse, she supposed it would be Raymond, somewhere between a view of Hell and a long stare at nothingness and an intermittent kaleidoscope whirl of pinnacles, minarets and stars. When he had taken her once into the quadrangle at All Souls he had made her lie on the grass to see the pinnacles of Hawksmoor's architecture against the profound sky of an Oxford evening turning towards night. Afterwards they had climbed the narrow stone staircase to his room, the scholar's study, with books and odd precious objects and sunlight from a high window.

'I suppose you will find the Philosopher's Stone,' she had said.

In the curious little room above, in the turret which was also part of his domain, there was nothing but a flute and a dusty guitar. Robert had said that Raymond should give dinner parties there; Raymond had seemed to like the idea. That had been before the number book, though. It might have been during the alternative medicine phase; those herbs which she still believed had been some help to her when she was depressed after Amy was born. Not that she had told Raymond she was depressed; she had found out which herbs to use without telling him why she was interested. She had never told Raymond anything, as far as she could remember. Or anyone else for that matter. Perhaps she had told Robert things occasionally; but Robert had a way of not hearing what he did not want to hear. It was one of his strengths.

When she had discussed engagements and invitations with Fiona for as short a time as was consonant with civility, Alison went upstairs to the little sitting-room looking over the Embassy garden and sat at her desk.

'I was a nervous child,' Raymond had written. 'I always did as I was told.' A thin child, dark-haired, growing up in the War in a Berkshire village, his father the schoolmaster, his mother dark-eyed and intense, singing 'Land of Hope and Glory' in the village church. Raymond had told Alison about that; his mother sang contralto and loved music and fussed over her only child. She cried when he was sent away to school, but never questioned it; and was proud when the reports came. A very able boy, they wrote of her delicate nine-year-old, undoubtedly scholarship material. She had not seen him in that light but was not surprised, she'd always known he had a vivid imagination. His tutor looked mildly surprised when she ventured this comment at some uncomprehending confrontation; it was mainly memory at that age, the tutor said, and a natural grasp of sequence. Certainly he had quickly grasped the sequence which made him Captain of Cricket, Head Boy and winner of the top scholarship to his public school. He once told Alison that no one who had been to prep school could fail to believe in original sin, but when she thought that sounded sad he said, 'I loved every minute of it.'

So this little top dog, alertly following the scent laid down for him, progressed from the sun-crowned peaks of one small world to the dreariest plains of a slightly larger one; a new boy, a low form of life. He claimed to have loved that too – 'Well, after the first couple of terms anyway.'

Alison, ten to his thirteen (not that she had known him then) had had a brown tweed skirt at the time, flecked with orange, rather prickly. The tailor in Wells had made it; it had two box pleats in the front and two behind and was cut in such a way that the front pleats began immediately below the curve of her stomach, with an effect, she felt, of fatal over-emphasis. The back was all right because the pleats began at the outermost point of her bottom and therefore diminished rather than accentuated it, but whenever she wore that skirt she was embarrassed by the front of it and by the way in which after she had been sitting down there were creases exactly where the pleats began and her stomach went in. She was not fat, either then or at any other time in her life, but it was true that her stomach was naturally slightly protuberant, never quite flat. That was how she remembered herself at ten, in the lumpy tweed skirt, anxious.

Her sisters had had skirts of the same tweed but they somehow looked different; perhaps it was because they were taller. The boys had had suits of a similar tweed, with knickerbockers for shooting; three boys and three girls, Alison the youngest, on the Somerset plain in the years immediately after the Second World War. The boys went away to school, the girls went daily to a school nearby, bicycling the five miles there and back through all weathers. Leaving the house they set off straight away up the unfinished cedar avenue planted by their great-grandfather, a mile of huge cedar trees ten yards apart, leading nowhere; at the end of the narrow road was a crossroads; equally narrow, equally unfrequented roads led left and right; if you went straight on you came eventually to the distant odd eminence of Glastonbury Tor. The great grandfather had had some grandiose plan for the apex of the avenue, a mausoleum or monolith, a piece of architectural bravado in defiance of his status as a younger son, only to abandon the whole project when his brother's wild horsemanship made him the heir after all and he moved a mile or two the other side of the village to the yellow stone house his family had held with no particular distinction for a century or so. Alison's father looked unlikely to follow; he had two elder brothers and was himself the least robust of the three. He concentrated instead on business, to the detriment of his never very considerable patrimony.

Neither parent was close to Alison; they had concerns of their own. The three sisters bicycled to school or stayed at home and messed about; there were two fat ponies. The boys came home in the holidays; sometimes they brought friends; there was tennis on the lumpy grass court or shooting over fields of turnips. In recollection it seemed that everything was the same year after year until Alison was eighteen. It was a long childhood; hard to grow out of.

Raymond had told her that he had been to Glastonbury when he was fifteen, in a bus from his school. Some romantic English master had taken his School Certificate class there to try to interest them in the legends of King Arthur because they were reading Tennyson's Morte d'Arthur. The boys were scornful, Raymond said. Mostly classicists, they thought the Matter of Britain boring stuff about ignorant barbarians, and the whole thing short on evidence. Perhaps Raymond exaggerated because when he told her he was trying to explain that there had been something wrong with his education.

'My desire to please,' he now wrote in his letter, 'overcame my capacity to think. My true critical faculty was dormant, though a false one was hard at work. I had not an original idea in my head.'

Alison wondered if anyone could reasonably be expected to be original at the age of fifteen, but she could see that Raymond was resolved to castigate himself. His handwriting, which was nervous but well-formed, showing traces still of the influence of that same English master, a proponent of the italic script, was beginning to wander up the side of the page; she wondered what mood he had been in, how quickly he had been writing, whether it had been late at night.

'They taught me certain codes,' he wrote. 'They taught me to be intellectually competent. They taught me nothing about how to be good. You may say, how were they to know that afterwards that would be the only thing that interested me?'

Alison laughed aloud. Raymond's reputation was not that of a man much concerned with goodness. Indeed he was one of the few people she knew whom she had more than once heard described as bad. 'A bad man,' one of Robert's more substantial colleagues had said only a month or two before. 'Brilliant of course.'

'Why bad?' Alison had asked.

'That poor girl, for one thing.'

It had been at some kind of official dinner; the man on her

other side had claimed her attention and she had not liked to ask which poor girl; she could think of at least three candidates for the description.

'I took in all that they told me,' he had written. 'I thought it was all there was. It seemed so easy.'

The world of school had seemed to him complete enough. He had only pretended detachment; in fact he had found the life entirely satisfying. 'Only one thing really matters,' he had written to his successor in some position of splendour within the hierarchy. 'For God's sake don't let the beaks start thinking they have anything to do with the way the place is run.' For he and his group wielded a power which was more or less absolute; they were admired and feared and envied by masters as well as by boys. Indeed in some cases masters as well as boys accorded them something not far short of adoration; it was the atmosphere, the emotional intensity generated among over a thousand young males who had not yet grown out of ardour. Raymond lived for his last year or two at school at a high level of intellectual and physical achievement. He affected scepticism but was a true believer at heart, generously giving his best endeavours, bringing honour to ancient cloisters within which his name was added to those, his like, who had preceded him over the past five hundred years. In ceremony after ceremony he was accorded what was felt to be his due, the approval of his elders, the map references for the way ahead; and learnt also about betrayal, and about what you could not expect of people, and about envy and malice, and cowardice, moral and physical, and snobbery, social and intellectual (he was possessed of both these last himself). Before going up to Oxford he travelled round Europe for several months, mainly on foot; he learned about vice, which had somehow passed him by at school, and luxuriated in loneliness and melancholy, experiences so new to him that they struck him at first most favourably.

'And all this time,' he wrote, 'you knew about nothing but bicycles and ponies and sisters. You have no idea how privileged you were.'

If room to breathe was a privilege, that she had had. Otherwise she rather thought she had suffered from neglect. Not that she had minded; but she suspected it had not prepared her for what followed. At one time her father, Ferdy, was away in London all week; he had decided to be a stockbroker. He developed an enormous enthusiasm for the workings of the City of London and would expatiate at Sunday lunch upon the money markets and the commodity exchanges and the latest company results, and how really all that sort of thing was quite easy to understand once you got the hang of it. His children found it boring, but some of his local friends and relations became quite excited and began to ask his advice on their investments. He quickly acquired a reputation for extraordinary shrewdness and there was a period of euphoria when Alison was about eight when shares in several companies performed according to his prognostications. Mid-Somerset happily took its profits and Ferdy talked of building a swimming pool. It all came to an end when something frightful happened to cocoa futures. The children were unconcerned; they preferred swimming in the disused quarry anyway. Alison remembered her mother murmuring more or less to herself while arranging flowers, 'Imagine not speaking to Ferdy simply because the monsoon is late in the Congo – really some people are too extraordinary about money.' It seemed it was held against Ferdy that he had not known about the monsoon in the Congo; his reputation for sharpness was lost, and replaced by a general view that he was unsound. He returned to the country and invested what was left of his capital in a local firm making lawn-mowers. For the next ten years this business was perpetually on the point of breakthrough; in the meantime the Bank Manager had to be kept calm and induced to continue his loan without requiring security other than the company premises, Ferdy's house and what was known as the Home Farm, which consisted of the stables of the house and the three cows who lived in the park. (Later Alison's mother bought some brown sheep.) Ferdy generally speaking took the affairs of Lawntex very seriously. He put on his dark City suit in order to convey an air of financial expertise when he went to see the Bank Manager, and he not infrequently spent sleepless nights worrying about staff troubles or the fact that the Managing Director was asking for more money (Ferdy himself was Chairman). Only occasionally when old friends from his Army days came to stay (he had been in the Army all through the War) would he admit that the saga of Lawntex had its comic aspects; his descriptions of its high moments of drama or near-disaster, and its escapes from bankruptcy, which resulted more often from some unexpected turn of events than from the wise decisions of its Chairman, would grow more hilarious as the evening wore on, often culminating in his recollection of the moment when he realized that his costings had been such as to mean that every time they sold a lawn-mower they actually lost money; howls of happy laughter would reverberate up the stairs to the children's bedrooms.

It was not until many years later that Alison realized how dogged by financial insecurity her early years had been, or how many bills had only finally been paid by her mother's selling a photograph to a magazine. Anne Graham had taken up photography some time before the War, and because she had a naturally good eye for the shapes and conformations of things, and because she was a slightly obsessional character, she had become an expert, and spent much time in the old pantry which she had made into a dark-room and from which she would emerge exhausted but triumphant with acid-stained hands and a number of beautiful black-and-white representations of the surrounding countryside and the life lived in it. During the War some of her photographs were used in a series of booklets on country life which were published under the aegis of the Women's Institute to encourage the directing of local skills towards the war effort and to act as a kind of celebration of the England that was presumably being fought for. These little books, practical, naive and oddly poetic, became collectors' pieces in due course. Alison had the whole series in her bedroom bookcase, tattered now, for they were only paper-backed; the economy standard paper had turned yellow with age. These faded landscapes of her youth, the misty plain, the straight dykes that crossed it, the mysterious tower-capped hill which rose abruptly from the middle of it, the avenue of giant cedars striding so decisively in the direction of nothing at all, the calm stone façades of the village houses, the lines of village women bending over the rows of potatoes, the uniformed Land Girls smiling behind a stolid herd of fat Friesian cows on their way to be milked – all these induced in Alison on the rare occasions when she looked at them a painful nostalgia caused rather by the close intimacy she felt with what they showed than because she remembered the years they brought to mind as being predominantly happy; she had not been a care-free child.

After the War, Anne Graham's photographs often appeared on the cover of *Country Life* or *The Field*; she would walk or drive many miles in search of suitable views. Alison could clearly remember the day when *Country Life* agreed to pay the cost of her petrol for some particular journey. Her mother had been gleeful. 'They're cracking,' she had cried. 'It'll be lunches soon, and a new camera and free Wellingtons. Wait till Harry Roberts hears this.'

Harry Roberts was a young Yeovil accountant in whom both Alison's parents placed enormous confidence. He had introduced them to notions until then quite unfamiliar to them, such as company cars and expense accounts; they had taken to them with enthusiasm, and a lack of moral scruple which was not at all what he had expected of the gentry. No one among his clients was keener to fiddle the books or cheat the income tax man. For a respectable young accountant with his way to make in the world the Grahams were something of a liability.

'It's a question of priorities,' Ferdy explained to him, admitting quite shamelessly to a false entry in the farm accounts. 'We've got to bring the girls out, don't you see.'

So Alison, the last of the girls, moved with her mother to her aunt's borrowed basement in Kensington and appeared at a number of cocktail parties and dances looking remote and ethereal and inwardly fighting with the growing certitude that as far as adult life was concerned she was going to be quite inadequate.

Raymond of course was in another world.

'Robert never really enjoyed Oxford did he?' Raymond wrote. 'He thought it was all rather infantile; he wanted to get on with real life. I didn't. I wanted to be admired. Admiration was easily come by in those days; the tilt of a hat could do it for you, an overcoat too big and too long, a silly laugh, a capacity to consume alcohol. We made of each other monsters and demi-gods, and turned our exploits into myths by the constant re-telling of them. I throve in the over-heated, self-regarding coterie which considered itself, which probably was, the elite of Oxford. I cast off my former earnestness and dedicated myself to frivolity. My preoccupation was only with style and not at all with content. I didn't believe in content, in the sense of anything verifiable and enduring. I felt we had been liberated from content. The great philosophers of the twentieth century had proved conclusively that nothing, nothing at all, could be called in any commonly understood sense of the word true. I felt that this gave me a glorious and dizzying freedom to be, say, do, feel, anything I liked; I was post-Wittgenstein man. Later on of course I saw that I had misunderstood Wittgenstein, and that most of my teachers had too. In the meantime I pranced about in full display; my mother would have called it showing-off. I saw very little of my parents, who bored me; and yet a good deal of what I did must I think have been done in order to shock them, or rather since they knew nothing about it, to shock that part of them that still remained in me. I was an odious young man.'

Alison remembered the odious young man quite well. It had been at about this time that she had first, briefly, met him. He had danced on a table in a house just off Park Lane, and knocked over some glasses and laughed wildly, and one of the young men had said quietly, 'Sir Percy's inane laugh,' and they had all groaned. It seemed this particular young man, who was of serious aspect, though handsome, was in the process of manufacturing a group joke. It had started as a comment on Raymond's laugh, and a reference to Baroness Orczy's Scarlet Pimpernel, whose most daring deeds had been preceded by his foppish laugh, and it was now trembling on the verge of becoming either a tremendous bore or quite disproportionately funny; the thing was in the balance. They were enjoying themselves more than anyone else, this particular group; and Alison and Charles Northcot, who often supported her by his silent presence on this sort of occasion and who later worked in the British Museum and later still (for she had seen him only a few years ago) virtually gave up speaking altogether, sat and watched them; and from a position of excluded hostility slowly relaxed into interested onlookers, feeding on the vitality of these strangers and re-assured by their apparent obliviousness of anyone other than their own group. Raymond was persuaded to come down from the table, food was brought, conversation moved rapidly though remained esoteric to the onlookers, and every now and then something or other was pronounced inane and attributed to Sir Percy. The breakthrough as far as the joke was concerned came when the serious young man looked dolefully at a plate which had just been put before him and pronounced it to be Sir Percy's inane kedgeree. Inexplicably Alison laughed as hysterically as everyone else except Charles Northcot.

'Oh we do have such fun!' Raymond cried, trying to get on the table again.

The anxious brother of the girl for whom the party was being given – James, in other words, the brother of Caroline – came to remonstrate, sent by his mother who had been on the lookout all evening for rowdiness from James's undergraduate friends. Raymond with much animation moved off with intent to charm the mother; he was only partially successful. She refused his invitation to dance but passed him over to her daughter Caroline. Alison, having by now taken to the dance floor with Charles Northcot, saw them approach, Caroline quite round of face and figure. 'She's hating it all you know,' Alison had heard someone say of her. 'She's a mathematical genius but her parents won't hear of it.' More than mathematical genius was needed to keep Raymond upright. The band – was it Tommy Kinsman's? – took it into their head, as they sometimes did at this stage of the evening, to play an old-fashioned waltz: there were one or two couples who appeared at every dance and were known to be expert. Raymond whirled round and round, coat-tails flying (for he was in white tie and tails), cheeks flushed, eyes bright, a lock of dark hair falling forward over his white forehead, round and round, and faster and faster, but Caroline though stolid as a pivot was not a tower of strength. She let him loose and he spun across the floor towards a substantial arrangement of potted palms and hydrangeas. He twirled into them like a tornado; the destruction was total. A few moments later he rose from the wreckage and holding one arm across his face like the chorus in a Greek tragedy stretched the other behind him and, more or less in time to the music, chassé-ed across the

115

floor and out of the room, down the stairs, across the hall and out into the night.

'What an odious young man,' said Charles Northcot.

*

Alison did not see Raymond again for some time, but the other one, the serious-looking one, was Robert, and he appeared at a dinner party a few months later, and differed from his host about the Government's policy over Suez. He did this with due deference to the older man, putting his points modestly and in the form of queries; but when the conversation became general and he turned to Alison who was sitting next to him he said abruptly, 'Sorry about that. They make me sick, those sort of people.'

Alison disliked politics. She preferred to think the people running the country knew what they were doing; any other idea was too disquieting to be entertained.

'I didn't know you were interested in that sort of thing,' she said. 'I associate you more with Sir Percy's inane kedgeree.'

It needed a good deal of explanation before he remembered. She supposed a lot of his evenings were like that.

'Not now,' he told her. 'I've got to work.'

'What about the other one? The one who kept getting on the table.'

'Raymond. He doesn't have to work. He can't fail to get a First whatever he does.'

'He didn't look that sort of person.'

'He does work occasionally as a matter of fact, at dead of night and that sort of thing. People think he doesn't. He encourages the myth.'

'And after these brilliant degrees? What will you do then?'

Robert was going to try for the Foreign Office but was wondering whether if he passed he would want to work for a Government with whose policies he disagreed; he took the problem very seriously. He thought Raymond would read for the Bar, make a lot of money as a barrister, go into politics and in no time at all be Chancellor of the Exchequer in a Labour Government.

'Goodness,' said Alison. 'First impressions can be very misleading.'

That was when Robert began to be interested in Alison. His interest had a good deal to do with the sound of her voice, and her flat delivery of the cliché, which gave it a slight ironical overtone, and the conformation of nose, one ear and neck which since he was seeing her in profile were the most observable of her features. In the course of the evening he asked her a number of questions about herself; she avoided them as best she could. He gave her a lift home in his car; she flinched at passing traffic.

'I'll have to see you again,' he said. 'You haven't told me anything.'

'There's nothing to tell,' she said again. She put her hand on his arm for a moment and said apologetically, remembering how men hated to have their driving criticised, 'As you can see my distinguishing characteristic is cowardice.'

She believed it. She could understand what seemed to her her hopeless nervousness, but she could see no point in denying it. Naturally she was stoical about it; anything else would be bad manners; but she could not assume a boldness she did not feel. The only living things which did not alarm her were plants, but when she suggested to her parents that she should get a job in a nursery garden near Glastonbury they said she would never meet anybody there.

'Who could you hope to marry?' they said.

Her mother went back to the country and Aunt Domenica returned to the basement flat in Kensington; Alison became her lodger and took a course in Cordon Bleu cookery. Later on she met a man who had a friend who had started a garden shop in W.8. He brought most of the plants up from his garden in Surrey, but Alison was happy enough in the yard behind the shop tending the pot plants and advising people on their window boxes or their newly built patios. Her parents, busy with Lawntex and photography and the leaks in the roof and the tortuous campaign against the income tax man, hardly took in the change from cookery to gardening; and Aunt Domenica was glad to have her window boxes regularly replenished with rejects. Behind the window boxes Aunt Domenica entertained curates to tea, and sometimes even an Archdeacon, for her life was dedicated to the infiltration of the Church of England by the highest of high Anglo-Catholic persuasion. Alison found this background of religious scheming comfortingly irrelevant. She felt that Aunt Domenica accepted her without question, not as she was, for no one knew her as she was, but as she ought to be.

'No one laid upon you the burden of their expectations,' Raymond wrote. 'You were never anyone but yourself.'

Alison felt this to be quite wrong. There had been expectations – but what had they been? That she should make a good marriage perhaps? And as for being herself, what was there to be proud of in that? Of course she understood that what was widely expected of Raymond was of quite a different order. With his First and his Fellowship of All Souls and his book commissioned by a publisher, it was to be presumed that he would continue to rise smoothly towards ever greater illustriousness. He presumed it himself.

'My only saving grace,' he wrote, 'lay in my drunkenness. I didn't know that. I thought I was drinking in the same way that I used to pretend not to work before exams, to show I didn't care, to show that the glittering prizes came to me in spite of myself, because of my brilliance, and not because I wanted them or worked for them. But that wasn't true. I was drinking because I didn't want to think. And that was my saving grace, because it showed that I knew I ought to think. But if that awareness ever came into my conscious mind – and I don't remember that it did – I should certainly have said to myself, not yet. I had other preoccupations. For instance, there was letting down Louise. That took up a surprising amount of my time. I wanted to do it really well. I have described to you the exhilaration of the discovery of intellectual doubt. The discovery of one's own capacity for emotional unreliability can be almost as exciting. I call it emotional unreliability rather than moral baseness because of course I didn't believe there was such a thing as moral baseness, but the sort of behaviour I am talking about is the sort of behaviour your father would have called caddish. "The fellow's a cad," your father would have said. I would have been proud to have acknowledged it. Louise, you may remember, was a serious girl. Or did you never know her? She was a few years older than you, I suppose, and the belle of Oxford. It was the fashion to be in love with her. She was tall and blonde and had blue eyes with dark lashes, and a light dusting of fair hair on the outer curves of her cheeks which were naturally high-coloured, 'a lovely young crea-ture' the old dons croaked as she sped by, always in a hurry, on her bicycle or running bare-footed – oh so many bad poems compared her to Atalanta. Of course she was spoilt. The ratio of women to men in Oxford in those days was still absurdly small and she came in for a lot of adulation. She could be funny too, and extremely rude when she wanted to be. She was also supposed to be clever, though there were several much plainer girls who were more so. But she was sharp, and incipiently tough. She wanted to be a writer. Later she became a good journalist, but in those days she wanted to write a great novel; when I was unkind to her she would say she supposed it might be good for her work, but I don't believe it was. Our affair was a power struggle. It was a long war, lasting more than two years, and in the end my victory was absolute. She lost all her pride, moved in with me (a much less usual thing for a girl to do in those days), did badly in her exams, longed for me to marry her. She ceased to be a challenge; I lost interest. I

119

began an affair with a girl called Jeanie, who was in Oxford to do a teacher-training course and to sleep with as many men as possible before going back to Aberdeen and her boyfriend, who was learning to be a doctor. I once sent her round to drop a note through the door of my lodgings when I knew Louise would be looking out of the window, waiting for me; the note said I wouldn't be back until the next day, giving no explanation. If you wanted to put a better construction on my behaviour you could perhaps say that I wanted to force Louise to be the one to end the affair, thus leaving her a little of her dignity. I have sometimes wondered whether all that feminist journalism she went in for in the 'seventies wasn't really addressed to me, even all those years later. Anyway, I read somewhere recently that she'd disappeared into a remote part of Asia with a Turkish poet so I daresay she's happy. "I see no reason for that conclusion," said the ambassadress in a dry tone. "Many people would find remotest Asia with a Turkish poet the opposite of a happy concept." Well quite. Anyway the next thing was I wrote my first novel, and more or less in that tone of voice. It was heavily influenced by the manner of Ivy Compton Burnett and the matter of Evelyn Waugh. One critic in a provincial paper dismissed it briefly as derivative and jejune. Excellent man. Everyone else clapped their hands and cried, "Oh what a clever young man!" I cried it myself every morning, looking into the mirror. As often as not I clapped my hands as well.'

*

Alison put down the letter on the desk in front of her – there were still many pages to read – and getting up from her chair went to the window and stood looking down at the orderly enclosed garden beneath her. How much of all this did Raymond mean? Had she ever known how much of what he said he meant? People's personalities shifted so, were different in different lights; one had always to make allowances. Raymond's defensiveness must be considered part of his personality, and yet she had seen him without it, and when she had seen him without it he had seemed easier to know completely than anyone else she had ever met.

It must have been about the time of which he was writing that she had seen him for the second time, again at a party. He had asked her why if she was a gardener her hands were not engrained with earth. She had told him she wore gloves. She had told him how she had been with Aunt Domenica to one of the midweek services at which with swinging censers and eager acolytes Father Featherstone administered the Eucharist according to rites as Romish as the Church of England could countenance, and there Aunt Domenica, whose hands were dutifully held before her to receive the host, had allowed her attention to wander to her niece's similarly cupped hands. Immediately the service was over she had decreed gloves for gardening.

'Every morning when I leave she bellows from her bed to remind me. I told her I was shocked at her frivolity in noticing my dirty hands when she should have been possessed with religious fervour but she said the spirit came and went but one could always have clean hands.'

They had walked round the garden. The party was being given in a house in St John's Wood and there was a garden big enough to have been laid out by an expert known to Alison. Raymond asked her the names of plants and talked about a garden near Oxford which had been laid out in the picturesque style for a house now ruined, and about imaginary gardens and the landscapes of dream. He did not talk about himself. Only towards the end of the evening, in the dark garden before going back into the house, he put his arms round her and holding her tightly laid his cheek on her head and said, 'How tired I am.' Then taking her gently by the shoulders he held her away from him and said, 'You're almost as thin as I am,' and touching her face with one hand added, 'But a great deal more beautiful.'

When she told Robert a few days later that she had seen Raymond he said at once, 'What did he say about me?'

'We didn't talk about you.'

'Why not?'

'I don't know. Probably he doesn't know you know me.'

'I suppose you thought he was terribly attractive.'

'Quite attractive, yes.'

Alison turned away from her contemplation of the Embassy garden, sat down again at the desk and picked up the letter. 'When I heard you were going to marry Robert I felt an acute sense of loss. Unjustified of course. I think I told even myself that it was Robert I was regretting, when it was you I mourned, whom I had come nowhere near to possessing.'

Alison threw the letter down on the desk and stood up again, more impatiently this time.

'We are forty,' she said angrily, walking up and down the room. 'Fifty. Robert is fifty, for Heaven's sake.'

The evening Robert had taken her out to dinner, the evening she had told him that she had walked in the garden with Raymond, the evening Robert said, 'What did he say about me?', that evening Robert had kissed her, and she had responded, not with the passive stillness which was all he had been able to elicit before nor with the casual affection or the occasional simulated fervour with which she was used to react to the young men who took her home after parties, but with a confident lack of reserve which firmly removed a number of barriers for whose collapse Robert had been expecting to have to negotiate a good deal longer. He had already decided to marry her. There were several good reasons. She was slightly mysterious to him; she was suitable on a number of conventional grounds; at the same time her reserve, her irony and her good taste made her more interesting than other girls of her background. His own age, his burgeoning career, his wish for a calm domestic background, all indicated marriage. The kiss marked a step forward. Alison considered then, in the darkness at the foot of the steps beside the terracotta pots full of white daisies, as she considered now looking down at the flower beds in the Embassy garden, that the fact that when she returned Robert's kiss she was thinking of Raymond was neither here nor there. If it had been the curious vitality of Raymond's thin frame against hers, the presence in his embrace of his intense existence, which had elicited the response from which Robert had the benefit, what purpose was served by anyone's knowing it? She admired Robert, had already recognized that his progress through the world, seeming as it did to have so much more purpose than her own, might be about to sweep her passively along with it. Raymond was quite different. It was simply not conceivable that Raymond could play any serious part in her life. She was much too much afraid of him for that.

*

'How did I come to stay on so long after your wedding, after you and Robert had driven away and the champagne had run out and the other guests had gone? Somehow I was still there the next day in my tail coat helping your mother disentangle the sheep from the rose bushes and heave them back over the fence into the park. I should have liked to have stayed still longer in that house where all the doors seemed always to be open and people wandered in and out, unhurriedly concerned with a number of disconnected purposes, and everything that was there, however casually disposed about the place, contributed to a sense of harmony, between objects, colours, shapes, even sounds. It was as different as could be from the conventional neatness of my own home. Besides, your mother's nose was like yours. But I went away and pursued my ambitions quite properly for all those years while you and Robert were in Rome and then in South America. I took my law exams, spoke at political meetings, started another book. When it became clear that it would be years before I could hope to get adopted as a Parliamentary candidate because my youth and fondness for flippant remarks made me suspect to the worthy citizens who sat on selection committees, and when it also became clear that it would be almost as long before I could make any money at the Bar, and when it also became clear – and this was the hardest to accept – that I was not going to be a good writer, whether as a novelist or a poet – I went into television. I went on with my book on seventeenth century science which took me fifteen years and is OK – by which I mean it is a contribution, quite a boring one but a perfectly worthy little stone in a perfectly decent edifice—but the money was in the media and off I went. I think for a moment I thought I had a mission to popularize the arts. The trouble was that all this time the picture I had of the world didn't fit, it was a model that didn't work, and though I was satisfied for a year or two with the superficialities of television and money and 'sixties trendiness it wore thin fairly quickly. So back I went to Glastonbury, with that dreadful old horse, do you remember? And you and Robert came and it poured with rain and we had to push the caravan out of the mud and Peg, pretty Peg you remember, got bitten by a drug-crazed Californian nose-flute player and thought she was going to get rabies. I remember you sitting, almost entirely concealed in that Mexican horse blanket you'd very sensibly brought with you, leaning against Robert with the firelight on your face, listening so attentively while I talked rubbish about the new awakening and alteration of consciousness and other fads of the moment, and at the end you said you agreed with it all, of course of course, you said, it's so funny. I hadn't exactly got involved in it for that reason – at least I don't think I had – but, well, yes, it was funny wasn't it?'

Alison remembered being completely happy: what was more, she had known at the time that she was completely happy. Her usual preoccupations had vanished, dissolved in the atmosphere which Raymond seemed to produce around himself at moments of high imaginative activity, an atmosphere to which she found it impossible not to respond with what felt like a quickening of the blood and was certainly a shouldering off of responsibility, a carelessness towards the logic of events if not of thought sequences, a recognition of the beneficence of the absurd and the munificence of the random. She and Robert had returned from two years in South America to find London a many-coloured market place in which most of their friends seemed to be stall-holders, crying, and wearing, their wares at one noisy, crowded gathering after another. Robert thought it amusing; Alison less so. By now she was in love with Robert and thought the new style allowed beautiful girls to be too forward in their approaches to married men. Among the hippies, sex, like everything else, seemed less competitive. Apart from the pot-smoking and Raymond's talk, being with them seemed much like the summers she and her brothers and sisters had spent sleeping out in make-shift camps in the woods. There was the same change of scale, the same concern with time-consuming minutiae, the same indifferent food produced with the same sense of achievement, the same woods and fields and streams and vanishing horizons. She found Raymond's new associates congenial. Their previous lives and their reasons for having changed them were so varied that the kind of categorizing curiosity which she was used to as part of social life seemed absent. Here one was accepted, not judged.

'I always thought a work of art would come out of all that,' Raymond wrote. 'I thought a phase of topsy-turveydom would send the blood to our brains. I thought the disenchantment with our inheritance, the supposed return to ancient wisdom, however impure the mish-mash of fact and fiction, vision and error, would make a fertile marsh out of which would come new life, a new myth. Of course I never thought King Arthur would come again, but

I thought someone might re-invent him. A poem, a story, a song, a painting, a statue, and off we could all go on some new tack. I suppose it was too weak, too amorphous; the trails were false, drugs, infantilism, the romance of violent politics – LSD, Hobbits, or the Socialist Workers Party. All those things involved the suspension of any kind of intellectual rigour and that was beyond me, though I daresay I killed a few hundred brain cells in my LSD phase.'

Alison had known less about that phase. Raymond had moved into a commune in North Wales; she and Robert had been to see him there once. The visit had not been a success. The place itself, though beautiful, was not welcoming. It was a big stone farmhouse surrounded by outbuildings. There were about twenty members of the commune but many of them seemed to be absent; the place had a desolate look. It had been a staging post for travellers on the old route from north-west Wales to London. Cattle drovers could have found shelter there, or merchants, or pilgrims, or spies. Among the outbuildings were the remains of a small chapel, but the design was unusual; the floor was round, paved with big stones laid in a circle; there was a local belief that it had been built in pre-Christian times. There were no trees close to the group of buildings, which stood on the bare hillside facing a view of great splendour, over mountains and green valleys and eventually the sea. In the overgrown vegetable patch behind the house there were quantities of herbs; Alison thought perhaps it was the preponderance of rue which gave the house its strange slightly bitter smell.

Pretty Peg who had been bitten by the Californian nose flautist had been displaced in Raymond's affections by Margery, who had been featured in a *Guardian* article on drop-out wives. She had a great deal of red-gold hair, clothed her statuesque figure in flowing green velvet and cowboy boots, and sang folk songs in a powerful contralto, with or without her own guitar accompaniment. Raymond took them for a walk in the evening; they saw a pair of peregrine falcons. He was smoking more marijuana than when they had last seen him and after the vegetable soup he smoked himself into total silence; Margery talked about education. Robert and Alison drove on the next morning with some relief.

'One thing about LSD was that sometimes sex was rather wonderful,' Raymond wrote. 'You were saving each other from the terror.'

Alison thought sex with Margery might have been a terror in itself. She turned the page quickly.

'The cumulative effect of drugs was bad for me. It manifested itself quite quickly and I had no trouble in giving them up, but for a time I thought the effect might be permanent. I was frightened. I think I was probably right to be frightened. I think I came to know something then which once you have known you are never quite free of. Dear Alison, in your calm and beautiful life you can't have known it – I mean despair, which is the sin against the Holy Ghost.

'Margery had a strong character, and when she was convinced she was right – which was often – she could be remarkably unbending. In fact I must say Margery was pretty foul to me most of the time, especially about money. Of course the whole commune foundered on money, the way most of these things do. Margery had put in more than I had – somewhere in the background was a Scottish laird for a grandfather – and she thought that gave her the right to be brought tea in bed in the morning and to let out a peremptory squawk every now and then which meant that I was to drop everything and rush to peel potatoes. If I didn't she would throw something at me, something quite hard, like a bucket. Why did I put up with it? I suppose because I was in such a low-spirited condition; perhaps because I believed the defrocked priest Evan when he told me it was good for me to be humiliated. It wasn't. I began to feel the pull of the downward spiral of dread, the accelerating spiral that swirls you down the plughole in the end; I ran whimpering back to my little room in All Souls and shut the door. She couldn't get me there; women weren't allowed in in those days. Even so I found myself unable to go out. There was only one other person on my staircase, a childlike professor of Greek who had spent his early life in Heidelberg. It would be impossible to imagine anyone less menacing and yet I went to extraordinary lengths to avoid meeting him on the stairs. I lurked in my room, gave it out that I was away, slipped out very early in the morning to buy food to last for several days. I tried to bury myself in work on the seventeenth century Science book. I had done all the research and half the writing; it was at a relatively easy stage, but some days I managed hardly more than one sentence, crossed out, re-written, corrected, cut, altered, over and over again. I tried to write about my despair because I thought if I could observe it I could distance myself from it, but day after day I found there was nothing I could say. It had gone beyond words. A blank page expressed it better. Sometimes I wrote down the physical symptoms in great detail, the heaviness of limbs, the semi-coma, the distended stomach, the headaches, the maddeningly irritated eyes, the extraordinary irregularities of the heartbeat during the night – but let's forget all that. I recovered. I was sick of impracticalities and of myself. I became a medical student. I arranged with the television people to commission me to do four programmes a year on anything I liked in order to subsidize my studies. I moved to London, and took a flat in Lambeth, to be near St Thomas's.'

*

Alison had not seen the flat in Lambeth, nor indeed witnessed the despair. Robert had been sent to Budapest for two years and Alison had come back from there to Somerset for Charlotte's birth. She could not now remember whether or not, when he had come back on leave after the baby was born, Robert had seen Raymond. She had not been interested. Her whole life had been given over to the care and contemplation of the child. Someone must have told her that Raymond had decided to become a doctor; she remembered that Robert had not thought that he would stick to it.

They went back to Budapest with the baby. Robert's career continued on its comfortable upward path; he had no complaint to make of the framework within which he found himself. He liked the formality – it was a game he understood – he liked knowing about policies from the inside, he liked the way it was accepted that for all his scepticism he was an Establishment man, he liked most of his colleagues, English and foreign, he liked the approaching prospect of ambassadorial rank. Alison played with the baby and did not concern herself with great matters. When they had leave, her sister Rosalind, the one who had not married, came out to help the Hungarian girl look after the baby; Robert and Alison went to Greece, and explored the Eastern Mediterranean.

After that Robert had an affair with Elsie Underwood, one of the secretaries at the Embassy.

Raymond had written that he was sick of himself. So had Alison felt towards the end of that bad time. Had she not had the bad time, or had she not lived through it, she might never have known herself. How much of a loss would that have been? But self-knowledge was supposed to be a good thing. Certainly she had come to know herself during that time, and then she had disliked herself very much, and then after all she had settled down with herself. Now though she tried not to think about it for fear the bad times might return, she would probably have to admit that she didn't mind herself at all; if only because she understood there was really no question and never had been of her being other than she was. She had pretended to be other than she was, for a time, in the early years of her marriage – or so at least she now thought. She had pretended to be the sort of person Robert would have liked to be married to. And then he had had the affair with Elsie Underwood and she had become again as she had been at ten, in the lumpy tweed skirt, with her brothers and sisters on the Somerset Plain. She had seemed to be thrown back to that, had thought she must start again and had found she needn't; twenty years dormant, the same self would do. It had not really merged with another's, that other's who had not wanted to be merged with; it returned to her surprisingly intact; only it took her several years to see it.

Elsie Underwood was a gentle clever girl whose mother was half-Indian, father a tea-planter; when she laughed she wrinkled her nose and looked like a skinny boy, but her mouth often turned down at the corners and then her dark eyes were lowered in apparent melancholy; she was not lucky in love. She fell for Robert as soon as she saw him. He took pity, was patronising, a man of the world; suddenly he fell in love. He was indignant; it was not what he had expected. His ambassador hinted, Robert bowed to necessity, Elsie was to be transferred away from proximity. As it was to end he saw no reason to go on being discreet; he almost wanted – altogether wanted – Alison to find out. He wanted her sympathy.

She did sympathize; but the effort of imagination it cost her to do so left her short of sympathy for herself. The memory of the long conversations they had had was still painful ten years later; she had had to discover how different his idea of marriage was from hers. Of course she did later understand that this idea of his was not as different from hers as she had thought it was, because some of his talk at that time had been bravado. Later too she thought his desire to have another child to cement the marriage was more sentimental, more conventional perhaps, than she would have expected of him. Not that she regretted it, but in retrospect it might have been easier for her to have waited longer. Being pregnant at the same time as trying to adjust to the idea that Robert saw nothing unreasonable in being what she could not see as other than unfaithful to her – for it emerged that Elsie was not the first – had been a strain. She had done, it, she had seen that the way he saw things was perfectly sensible, that monogamy was an odd idea, that love meant different things to different people.

'Would you mind then, if I had affairs?' she had asked.

'Very much. But it is a risk one has to take.'

'I wouldn't take it. I mean I wouldn't take the risk of having affairs myself. If I fell in love with someone else I should be off, away over the fields in my bare feet, to the raggle taggle gypsies.'

'Then I hope you won't. Why would he be a gypsy?'

'He just would I think.'

Robert was grateful. He was also moved, because he saw in the early days how very much it hurt her; at least he thought he saw. In fact she concealed a good deal of the pain; she thought it excessive. She thought she could esti-mate how much pain such an episode was owed – a lot, she thought, but not as much as she gave it. She had allowed herself to believe she only existed in the light of Robert's love. That light was not removed but it was a different light, and for a time she could not see herself in a different light, and was afraid she might not be there at all. And then eventually this other earlier self had materialized in the empty space at which she seemed perpetually to be anxious-ly staring, this childish but solid figure, feet on the ground, hands full of grass or leaves, concerned with the feeding of some prosaic beast; she had after all a fundament, was more than a mere impulse of pain at loose in the meaningless flux of an endless universe. She judged herself harshly. She condemned herself for having called what she now con-sidered her former state of neurotic dependence on Robert by the name of love; in her determination not to fall into self-pity she fell briefly into self-hate. Amy's birth was difficult. Afterwards Alison held her through many night hours weeping and confessing 'I don't love you, I don't love you at all.' Robert knew nothing of that, but he saw her drooping, falling back on the mechanism of habit to pilot her through the days; he was kind and considerate. When Raymond suggested himself for a visit, Robert wrote at once to encourage him.

'How separate our distresses are,' Raymond's letter continued, referring to that visit. 'What right had I to ask about something which you so evidently had under control – at least I think you had. Robert said you had not been well. Was that all it was? You were veiled from me by the mysteries of motherhood, which I did not understand. I thought perhaps he meant that you had looked at death, which I did not understand either, although by that time I knew its face. The happiness of the days we spent together was oddly enhanced by your melancholy, and by the way in which it fled in the daytime and closed in again in the evening. I had always thought there were things about you that Robert could never understand. I thought so even more then, though he was kinder to you than I had ever seen him. Was that because you had endangered yourself to bear his child? All that is an unknown area to me. We went far into the country, across the huge cornfields and into small active villages in one of which there was a fair. The three of us talked a great deal. Perhaps you and Robert missed old friends among the circumscribed samenesses of diplomatic existence. You both seemed so pleased to see me. In the daytime when Robert was working you and I walked by the Danube or looked at churches or sat in cafés and talked. I think you have always encouraged me to talk too much. I told you about the programmes I was making on herbs and remedies. You even took notes about some of the herbs. And then when you came back to England you made a herb garden; I was so pleased about that.'

The herb garden had been in the small space behind the house in Chelsea; two years in London had followed the time in Budapest. Raymond had seen it at its earliest stage and under his influence Alison had turned it into a maze, a simplified version – so he assured her – of one designed by the magus Dr John Dee himself for Queen Elizabeth of Bohemia in 1607. In her search for the plants she needed she renewed her old gardening contacts and before long had been drawn in in a consultative capacity. She began to earn money, took a day course in business management, discovered or encouraged growers of various generally forgotten species, and was written up in a shiny magazine. Since her natural inclination, combined with slight laziness and the fact that she only worked when the children were at school, meant that she turned down more than half the commissions she was offered, she soon became much sought after and on Robert's advice put up her prices.

*

'I had lunch with Robert at his Club one day and he told me that I was beyond a joke,' Raymond wrote. 'Putting all that effort into becoming a doctor at your age and then not practising – you really are becoming beyond a joke.' I explained that I thought it might come in useful in a revolution; he didn't think that funny. My seventeenth century book had just come out and he wanted me to concentrate. It was called controversial – in other words some of the professional historians expressed outrage though most responded very well. Robert thought I ought to join in all the back-biting and become part of the academic hierarchy. He couldn't understand that that was the last thing I wanted. I thought he was pompous, he thought I was irresponsible, just as we had always thought of each other; only since we were now in, or in my case approaching, our forties, I suppose we were becoming closer to the stereotypes, and at the same time of course, more inflexible in our prejudices. Robert said in that case why couldn't I become a proper novelist . . . Did he mean by a proper novelist one who produced a book every two years, made money by selling the film rights, was asked to appear on television panel games? . . . Well, but what was wrong with that? . . . Nothing, except that I couldn't do it . . . You could do it better than so-and-so and so-and-so and so-and-so . . . But I am not interested in doing it, my idea of a novelist's life is a different idea, a childish idea, an old-fashioned idea . . . Explain please . . . It is childish because it entails making up stories in the same way as we dream dreams, or rather not in quite the same way because being a waking dream it involves the will, but using those same mental processes, which in most adults are atrophied, or rationalized out of existence, except in sleep. I believe they can only be kept open by practice, by exercise, and unless you start young the atrophy sets in and there is nothing there to exercise. You can imitate it easily enough but it won't be the real thing. I imitated. I didn't start young enough. Secondly my idea of what a novelist should do is an old-fashioned one, because I think that each work should be a step forward from the last, that he should never repeat himself, that he should only produce a book when he is ready to add to his own knowledge – why write down what one knows already? – he should address himself to his generation, applying himself with a pure heart and humble mind to their legitimate question What Then Must We Do? (This is my favourite title – it's Tolstoy's as you probably know – he gave it to a little book about poverty in Moscow in the 1880s but I think it should be the sub-title of every novel.) The novelist should write for his generation and his concern should be nothing less than How To Live, but I do not know my generation and I haven't the faintest idea how to live. I explained all this to Robert and of course he understood perfectly. Having started off in mutual sus-picion – each thinking the other's life an implied criticism of his own – we ended up as friends, as we always do. "Oh and of course, love to Alison," I expect I said.'

If Raymond was talking about pictures of the world again (sometimes Alison was not sure what he was talking about) she supposed her picture might have constituted some kind of technique for survival by being so small. It hardly extended beyond a garden wall, or beyond the concerns of Charlotte and Amy. She no longer strained her imagination to encompass Robert's world though she remained pleased to see him when he came into hers. At the time of which Raymond was writing Charlotte and Amy were good little girls at Junior School, interesting and cheering, presenting almost no problems; Alison could hardly believe there had been a time when she had thought she could not love Amy. Amy was the livelier and more amusing of the two; Charlotte the responsible elder sister. They liked Raymond, but did not see so much of him after he went to live in Wiltshire, in a co-operative.

'It was going quite well – agricultural produce (market gardening really) combined with carpentry (pine kitchen cupboards). I'd been working on a historical programme about co-operatives. I'd lost interest in the seventeenth century by then, except to the extent that all that splendid ferment of ideas under the Commonwealth – Levellers, Diggers, Fifth Monarchy Men – had set me thinking about the re-emergence of some of them two hundred years later. Anyway I wanted to see something of the kind in practice. I thought anything, however miniscule, which could offer an alternative to the accepted management/labour demarcation could only be a good idea. I went to this place in Wiltshire which had been going for some time, but oh my goodness me, Alison, it was boring. I approved of it of course, I did a little study of it for a serious weekly, I worked quite hard picking fruit, theoretically I quite believed in the value of it all, but it was like one imagines a progressive boarding school, and though one of the people running it was quite intelligent and understood about business (in fact I think he later on infiltrated the place with his own relations and turned it into a successful family firm) most of the other people were really quite silly, and in the end I behaved badly, very badly. I ran away with the Vicar's wife. Now that was enormously foolish of me. And I only did it in order not to run away with the wife of the local landowner, whom I preferred. Pam Pargeter was her name, my preferred one's. You wouldn't have liked her. She used to slap her jodhpurred thighs and shriek with laughter at the slightest thing. She was pepetually sun-tanned, gleaming with health, bursting with energy, good humour, appetite for life. You'd have shrunk into your corner, pale and appalled. She was a jolly good sort, terrific on a horse. Her husband was quite a good sort too, an incipient alcoholic, too lazy to be a good farmer but quite knowledgeable about agricultural matters. Shooting was his passion. Pam's shooting lunches were famous. "You live the life of ideas," she said to me. "You don't care about people." I was relieved that she didn't call me selfish. I was her tame intellectual; there were the dogs, the horses and me. She was contentedly sensual. They spent a good deal of their time arranging their affairs so as to enable them to have more fun; their life was a succession of treats. They loved spending money. What a whey-faced, conscience-stricken schoolmaster I felt myself in comparison. Of course they were philistine and materialistic and rather crude, but then my own sensibilities were in danger of being over-refined – or let's say that I persuaded myself of that for a time, perhaps because I so much appreciated the escape to material comforts from the austerities of the co-operative life. And then I ran away with Bella Mackintosh.

'Pam thought I stood for something she'd just had a glimpse of every now and then, something Roger would never understand, something tremendously desirable. She'd have been dreadfully disillusioned if she'd put it to the test. She was a determined girl though, and I was becoming alarmed. I thought it would seem more final if I left with another woman rather than just making a run for it on my own. And Bella was desperate to get out.'

Ever since his undergraduate days Raymond had had the reputation of being unscrupulous in affairs of the heart. Alison had assumed that his increasing tendency to become involved only with women who were for one reason or another unlikely to be marriageable was to be accounted for by his unwillingness to be tied down by the obligations and regularities of married life. She had come to take it for granted that his emotional entanglements, being either ephemeral or with married women or, in one instance which she seemed to remember as having lasted longer than most, with an Icelandic air hostess, would be, not purposely concealed from her, but relegated to an area of his life which she would be unlikely to come across. Since he was obviously attractive to women she had assumed that he had not married because he did not wish to marry; it seemed in keeping with his general slight evasiveness. His appearance of having such matters more or less under control did not invite curiosity. Certainly she had never discussed anything of the kind with him except in the most light-hearted of manners. She wondered now how defensive on his part the light-heartedness had been.

'Bella's husband, the Reverend Kenneth Mackintosh, was really quite a nasty man. Suspecting it himself, he became a Christian. Suspecting again that that might not have done the trick, he became a clergyman, and remained haunted by the fear that God wasn't fooled. His nastiness lay in his selfishness, greed, deviousness, complete absence of generosity in thought, word and deed, the usual sort of thing; only he himself thought it lay exclusively in his sex urge. This did indeed seem to become increasingly hard to control. According to Bella there was nothing unusual at first, but after a few years of marriage it emerged that he

137

liked being beaten, and then it seems one thing led to another and his demands became more bizarre and more excessive and finally one day when he was on his knees praying and supplicating while she was hard at it pinning safety pins into his bare bum he turned on her with violent reproaches for her lack of interest in her work, and she rebelled; she said she wouldn't do it any more. After that he became unreasonable, wouldn't take no for an answer, took to making unexpected pounces when she was preparing the Mothers' Union tea. I am not making this up – people's lives are very peculiar, you know. Anyway somehow I allowed her to tell me about it – she'd never mentioned it to anyone before – and of course I was sorry for her. What was she to do? She had no money. Her parents were dead, her only sister was married and lived in Australia. Bella herself had married from teacher training college without finishing the course. If she left him against his will how was she to earn her living? The only thing she could do was keep house, and she wasn't very good at that. So you could say I offered her my protection. In return for her protection against Pam Pargeter. I rented a small cottage in a village just outside Oxford. I wasn't there much during the week because I was involved with various television projects; Bella enrolled at a secretarial training place in Oxford. Unfortunately her husband found out where she was and pursued her with reproachful letters and crazy telephone calls. The press took up his cause briefly – anything scandalous to do with Vicars is good for a laugh – and she and I came in for a bit of slander. He was even quoted as saying that I had seduced her away by witchcraft, which kept the reporters hanging hopefully round our front gate for a day or two. Then he said I'd written him a blasphemous letter. That was because I foolishly answered his ravings by writing him a long letter explaining that I thought he ought to reconcile himself to the idea that he and his wife were incompatible, and cheer up. I said I'd always wondered how he could be so gloomy when he belonged to the Church of Thomas Traherne – 'You never enjoy the world aright till the sea itself floweth in your veins, till you are clothed with the heavens and crowned with the stars . . . till you can sing and rejoice, and delight in God, as Misers do in Gold . . . etc. etc.' I suggested long country walks and a bit more ecstasy. It went down tremendously badly.

'I don't know what I should have done. I never had an affair with Bella. I liked her and was sorry for her. She wasn't very pretty; she had a face like a hare and was always blinking. Later when she calmed down she became better looking, a tamed hare, only occasionally wild-eyed. When the fuss died down we lived quietly in the cottage. She was a sort of unpaid housekeeper to me when I was there. There was mutual gratitude and friendship between us. She was happy to be free. She gradually became less shy and made friends with other people on her course. Everyone liked her; she's a nice woman. She has a job in Oxford now. In fact she runs the secretarial agency she went to work for; she's well-paid, efficient, has a nice little flat, rejoices in her freedom and independence. I take her my typing. I suppose she's one of the few people I see regularly and who knows me well.

'You could say it had a happy ending, but the whole experience was lowering. I'd made a fool of myself, left bad feelings. I felt isolated. There was no one I knew well enough to feel that they actually knew what I was doing, knew what my feelings, motives, reasonings were. You and Robert were abroad again by that time, Robert was Mr Ambassador at last. You'd been claimed by that official world I had no part in. The television projects all faded out; money was short, they said. It began to appear to me rather clearly that I had mucked things up. I was getting on for forty-five and I had no idea what to do next.'

★

When Robert first became an Ambassador he surprised Alison by revealing a strain of intense irritability which she had never noticed in him before. A confident and critical second-in-command, he became as head of the mission unexpectedly anxious, even – though this was known only to Alison – indecisive. When there was a decision to be made – even a minor question of staff changes or the requirements of protocol in connection with a visiting Government Minister – there would be several days of outward resolve and inward torture, revealed to Alison when they were alone by a quite unfamiliar snappishness about small domestic details. She was so accustomed to thinking of his work as something absolutely within his range and under his control that at first she suspected these symptoms of being connected with some aspect of his private life, a particular impatience with herself, or with someone else not known to her, and it was not for some time that she decided the trouble was simply nervous. She noticed how his upper lip sweated on important occasions and how his hand shook as he poured himself out a whisky and soda after some personage or other had left. On one such occasion she suggested he should worry less, on the grounds that nothing that the British Ambassador did in such an extraordinarily unimportant South American country as the one in which they were could have more than the most miniscule effect on the course of world events. He was so angry that he threw his glass on the floor and shattered it.

'You have never supported me,' he said. 'A man has a right to expect his wife to support him in his work, not to sneer at it.'

She had not meant to sneer, she said, rather to reassure.

'One thing you have never been,' he said. 'Reassuring.'

She went to bed in a state of high self-justification, but during the night decided he was right; he had a right to expect her support. She applied herself to the better organization of the domestic routine and to the memorizing of a number of small facts, incidents, names, with which he was supposed to be familiar and which he frequently forgot. From being thought of as a slightly unknown quantity, a little aloof, even – some had wondered – a little to be pitied, she became in the general view, without losing a certain remoteness, a person to be relied upon, for goodwill, for tact, for just that kind of wifely support of the absence of which he had complained. It came to be accepted that the Ambassador depended very much upon the Ambassadress. Robert was grateful. In earlier times she would have appreciated that. Now she might rather have been taken for granted, as being more peaceful.

'At forty-five,' wrote Raymond, 'it is not amusing to drink too much, nor to get into scrapes. "Been in any more scrapes lately?" says the Warden of All Souls, creaking like an ancient crane at his own facetiousness. "No, no, Warden . . . blameless life . . . terribly boring . . . hiccup . . ." Hate . . . spleen . . . flatulence . . . fear . . . You and your like, you foul old man, have sat sniggering over the naughtier passages of Catullus while those to whom you handed over the world of ideas have dethroned our species from the centre of the universe where once we sat, destroyed the god we made in our own image, demonstrated the meaningless-ness of our philosophies and the ineffectiveness of our institutions, shown us instead the infinite vacancy of space and the infinite pettiness of socialism – and then you ask us if we have been in any more scrapes lately. If I could find a scrape I'd climb into it whimpering, like a child getting into bed at the end of a bad day. The best I can manage is to tease my Bank Manager when he writes me letters about my overdraft.

'When I began this letter I promised myself there should be no self-pity in it. I'll return to the bare record of fact. My Bank Manager had every reason to be displeased; I had tried gambling on the Stock Exchange because I thought it might be better than making bad television programmes. The good ones I wanted to make were turned down for being too expensive. I thought if I could make some money I could finance the programmes myself. I found I had started taking money seriously too late; I was simply no good at it. In the meantime I was studying mathematics again. If through the inadequacy of my poetic gift I had failed to find a verbal key to the code I wanted to crack, perhaps I could get there by using another language, a wordless one. A significance of numbers might prefigure a significance of forms, perhaps of sounds, perhaps the music of the spheres . . . well, something of the kind.

'Then we met in that garden, do you remember? And I told you what I was working on, and you looked pleased, and I remembered how some time before I had taken you and Robert up to my room and you had said in that dreamy way you have, I suppose you will find the Philosopher's Stone. I saw for a moment very clearly, as it might have been in the background of a Renaissance painting, a tiny picture of my scholar's life as you saw it, my books and my table, the little window and the distant hills, and on the white road leading towards the hills past the tall cypress the tiny figures of a man on a horse, a flock of sheep, a party of travellers. It was because I despised myself for not telling you then how untrue that was that I later behaved so badly.'

He had behaved badly, that was undeniable. He had come to dinner with Rose and Malcolm Brewer, with whom Alison and Robert were spending the weekend, and he had behaved very badly indeed.

★

Rose was Alison's elder sister and Malcolm was her husband. They had four children. Malcolm owned an engineering business in the West Midlands. He had been rich, and now was less so. They had a small dairy farm which was more Rose's concern than Malcolm's because Malcolm had very little time to spare from running his business, which was his chief interest and pleasure. Indeed he could talk of little else, and he and Alison usually found themselves running short of conversation, though she always insisted to her sister, not quite convincingly, that she did not find him boring. That weekend Rose had explained rather defensively that Malcolm was having trouble with his business.

'It was too dependent on the car industry,' she said. 'It upsets him very much.'

Certainly he seemed preoccupied, and had lost weight.

'He's had to lay off people who've worked for him for years. He won't rest until he gets it right and can start taking people on again. He won't listen when I say it's just the recession and not his fault. He works much too hard.'

Raymond could not have been expected to know all that, because he had never met Malcolm before. To him he was probably just a rich businessman, easy game. Or perhaps he was nothing at all, because perhaps Raymond was not noticing people that evening.

It was Malcolm and Rosie's undergraduate son Hector who insisted on taking Raymond back to dinner with his parents. He was delighted to find that Alison and Robert were old friends of Raymond's. Some other young people from Oxford were coming to dinner; they were all, Hector said, mad about Raymond. Robert and Alison had not realized to what extent Raymond had become a fashionable, if elusive, Oxford figure.

'It isn't good for him,' Alison said. 'It makes him silly.'

'It wastes his time,' said Robert.

Robert was not in a good temper. Charlotte and Amy had come out from school for the afternoon. Robert had told them about his new job, and considered that they had been insufficiently impressed.

'It's just that they expect it,' Alison said. 'They expect you to go from one Ambassadorship to the next getting more and more important all the time. They're not surprised, that's all.'

She knew it was not quite all. She knew they were too concerned with their own affairs to be much interested in their father's career. After all they would probably be Ambassadors themselves quite soon. Charlotte would certainly do perfectly well as an Ambassador already. Probably she would be Head of the Foreign Office. Amy would be Lord Chancellor; she had decided to read Law. In the meantime they told Alison the school gossip, and she listened, because she found it interesting, and sometimes amazing, and sometimes indeed hard to credit, because the girls, recognizing an appreciative audience, exaggerated grossly. Robert did not find it interesting. He resented the fact that when Charlotte and Amy were there Alison listened to them and not to him. Alison found this unreasonable. She had noticed that he seemed increasingly to want her to listen to whatever he might want to say at whatever time of the day or night he wanted to say it, and she had noticed in herself an increasing reluctance to do so, sometimes because she had heard it already, sometimes because she disagreed, and sometimes because she wanted to do something else. She regretted this reluctance on her part but could not control it. His reaction to it, when he sensed it, was to talk more rather than less; it was as if he were claiming his right to do so. Sometimes she found herself leaving the room as soon as he came in so as not to give him the chance to start. The problem had never been discussed between them and it was unlikely that it ever would be.

On the evening that Raymond came to dinner with Malcolm and Rose, Robert had driven the girls back to school, which was some twenty miles distant. After the lunch party and the irritating tea at which Alison had paid so much more attention to the girls than to him, he was tired and out of humour, which was a pity because otherwise he might have been able to do something about Raymond. On the other hand perhaps nothing could have been done about Raymond.

He was drunk when he arrived, but not noticeably so except to those who knew him well. His face was pale, except for a bright patch of colour just below each cheekbone. He seemed to be swept into the room by the supporting young admirers, themselves excited and slightly hysterical, watching for a sign from him as to which way the evening was to go, waiting for his performance. He moved away from them, sat down to talk to Rose, accepted a drink from Malcolm. The audience waited; there was no question of their giving up. At dinner he responded to their prompting and began to talk rather wildly. He became malicious about characters not known to Malcolm and Rose, who were not amused. Aware that he was not holding all his audience, he became more outrageous, broke into imitations, funny enough, but for insiders only. Malcolm and Rose were not insiders. Raymond suddenly began an attack on modern industry, a confused diatribe against stupid managers and snobbish attitudes in the Universities which produced nothing but a proliferation of Civil Servants. Whenever Malcolm found anything with which he could begin to agree, Raymond would veer off onto another tack.

'Look here, you know,' said Malcolm. 'I mean, you simply haven't done your homework.'

Malcolm's son Hector became embarrassed, was afraid his father would make a fool of himself, tried to change the subject. Raymond was incapable of listening. Alison thought that if he stopped talking he might fall off his chair; she half-hoped he would. Robert tried to intercede but made no impression. Rose began to look depressed.

Suddenly one of the girls said, 'Oh Raymond, didn't you say you had to go and meet your Aunt Gwendolen?'

Raymond stopped in mid-sentence.

'Aunt Gwendolen?' He looked confused.

'Yes, yes. You know. You had to meet her at the station.'

For some reason he looked quickly towards Alison. Then he said firmly. 'No. Not Aunt Gwendolen. Not tonight.'

'Yes, yes,' they insisted, getting to their feet, impelling him towards the door. 'She'll be waiting for you.'

Robert stood up. 'In that case I'll drive you.'

One of the girls said her car was just at the door. They left. Alison went into the kitchen to help Rose with the coffee.

'I'm sorry about Raymond. It's just as well he's left.'

But before they had finished drinking the coffee, Aunt Gwendolen arrived. She said she had come by taxi from the station, though they had heard no car. She was wearing a full-skirted red taffeta evening dress, very high heels and an extraordinary feathered hat. She bore an uncanny resemblance to her nephew.

'The stupid boy hadn't turned up so I took a taxi,' she said. 'He told me he was dining with some divine people he'd just met.'

Rose offered her coffee, Malcolm suggested a glass of port.

'A teeny port would be quite gorgeous,' she said, proceeding not very steadily towards the sofa. 'Goodness you are sweet.'

Alison was astonished; she watched in silence. Then she quietly asked Robert if he had ever seen this before.

'Not for about thirty years. It used to be funny.'

'I suppose it still is.'

'Not in the context.'

For Rose and Malcolm, though surprised, were not incredulous. They suspected something, but not the truth. They were perfectly victimized. Robert and Alison would have liked to disenchant them but their own initial amazement had left them speechless long enough for the illusion to have taken hold. It was as if they had to waken two sleepwalkers. It seemed a long time before Rose suddenly clapped her hands and said that she had never laughed so much in her life, she'd known all along, well she hadn't really, but she'd thought there was something, and anyway it was terribly funny wasn't it Malcolm, and Malcolm said, 'Terribly funny,' looking completely mystified.

'You see who it is?' Rose laughed.

He didn't see.

'Come on, darlings, let's sing,' cried Aunt Gwendolen, jumping up and going towards the piano.

The young people followed; one of them sat at the piano. This was clearly something that had happened many times before. Aunt Gwendolen leant heavily upon the piano and began to sing, 'Come into the garden Maud,' in a bold falsetto.

Rose whispered to Malcolm. Malcolm listened without expression. Then he nodded.

'I see,' he said shortly.

A few moments later he quietly left the room. Alison looked questioningly at Rose. Rose shook her head. Aunt Gwendolen staggered and was propped up by two of the young men.

'Land of hope and glory,' they urged.

'Tired, too tired.'

The girl at the piano had started to play.

'Too tired, too drunk. Too drunk.'

The pianist played more quietly. The others had started to hum. Raymond sang. Clearly his audience had expected the falsetto. This time he forgot it. He sang in his own voice, a reedy tenor, perfectly in tune. He sang quietly, standing straight, with one hand on the top of the piano and the other on the shoulder of a rumpled young man a good deal taller than himself who stood beside him. His face was by now quite white, his feathered hat had slipped to the back of his head so that his greying hair fell over his forehead. A streak of the lipstick he had worn earlier still adhered to his upper lip. He gazed steadily in front of him and sang 'Land of hope and glory' as if it were a lament for the fallen. Then he slid to the floor in a heap of crimson taffeta.

Alison went upstairs to bed. Later she was woken by a loud crash from downstairs. Later still Robert came to bed.

'What was the crash?'

'Raymond knocked over a lot of china.'

'Has he gone?'

'They put him to bed.'

She woke early, as she had meant to do, and went downstairs to clear up. The early morning sun revealed no trace of the previous night's adventures. The silent house was perfectly clean. She went into the kitchen. The door was open, letting in sunlight and a smell of damp grass and, when he heard Alison in the kitchen, Rose's dog, a brown and white lurcher. Alison made some tea, and sat at the kitchen table in the sun to drink it.

Raymond appeared quite silently, because of his habit of wearing what Robert called gym shoes. He looked much as he always did, if a little pale. He helped himself to tea and sat opposite her at the table. They looked at each other.

'I'm too old for that sort of thing,' he said.

Alison nodded.

They sat in silence.

'Nice dog,' said Raymond.

'Very nice.'

They smiled.

After some time Raymond stood up and took a Sainsbury's carrier bag from beside the dresser.

'Some of these pieces are worth mending.'

He paused at the door.

'I'll write to them.'

★

'I walked all the way back to Oxford. It was a summer Sunday morning, as you will remember. There was no one much about. As I came into Oxford the church bells were ringing and I felt like Jude the Obscure. That's not true. I thought of Jude the Obscure but I felt almost nothing, by which I mean something so positive that perhaps I should say I felt almost everything. I was hardly myself, I was free of myself, absorbed in something other, something entirely beneficent, part of beneficence itself. I had taken that from you, sitting opposite you in the kitchen of the house where I had disgraced myself.

'So there we are. This is the end of my True Confession. Insofar as it is a declaration of love I make it for both of us. We love each other. You may never have admitted it to yourself – that I don't know – but I know that it is true. To the extent that I am also making a confession of failure that confession is mine alone. All of my life has been mis-directed. As a very young child I was near enough to reality to have set out on the right path had I been left to my own devices. As it was I was picked up and set down firmly on another path. I looked back only once, and saw you, standing at the place where the paths diverged. Then I went on in the way on which I was set. By the time I realized that I wanted to retrace my steps, you had gone. Consequently all my attempts to turn aside were doomed to failure. Of course they were perfectly good fun – some of them any-way – my life hasn't been too bad at all, don't think I am complaining. Only there isn't any point in it now that I know there isn't any point. I shall never find a picture of the world into which I can fit the pieces I seem to have been born holding in my hand, a patch of blue sky, some grass with unfamiliar flowers in it and a piece of someone's foot. Mathematics can't help me any more than anything else. Either the picture isn't there or I am not clever enough to find it. I'm not very clever you know. I don't know why anyone ever thought I was. All I have is enough busy mechanical apparatus in my head to confuse the real issues and make it impossible for me to re-invent the picture for myself. Anyway I'm off. Out of it. Into anonymity. I used to have a dream sometimes. I would be standing in front of a huge blank impassable wall, and then I would see an unexpected door, and it would open. You would be there, on the other side. I would go through the door, and we would take each other's hands, and look into each other's faces, without fear. I used to think even then that perhaps the door was death. I shall soon be fifty and the one road I am determined never to travel again is the one which spirals downwards.

'I wonder if my father got it right? I despised him, for being no more than a village schoolmaster, speaking with a country accent, collecting fossils, singing in the choir, looking for butterflies . . . Oh no, no, we would have done it better than that. Why didn't you tell me? You knew. You could have told me. Before you committed yourself to Robert, before the children were born, before you took on those obligations which I knew you better than ever to question, you could have told me. You could have told me the highest ambition I could have had would have been to live in love with you, to work at some humdrum activity so that we could buy bread – and wine to make glad the heart of man and oil to make cheerful his countenance – and live like Abraham and Rebecca, and never give in, and never come down from the mountain, and live all our lives in necessary industry and unnecessary joy; we could have done it. If you had told me, in that first garden we ever walked in together – but no, we were afraid.

'By the time this reaches you you will know what I have done. This is to tell you why. Also to send you what you have always had, my love.'

Alison ran through the Embassy calling for Robert.

'He had a luncheon engagement,' said Fiona reprovingly, popping out of her office.

Shaking her off, Alison hurried on to the nearest telephone and rang up her sister Rose in England. Had she heard anything of Raymond? Had there been anything in the papers? Would she find out if anything had happened to him, please with the utmost urgency would she ring back as soon as possible. Late in the afternoon Rose telephoned to say that no one had seen Raymond for several days. His room was locked.

Robert came back. Alison persuaded him to ring up the Warden of All Souls and have Raymond's room unlocked. It disclosed nothing unusual.

Robert read Raymond's letter. Alison waited. It seemed to take him a long time.

'Did you talk to him about me?' Robert asked.

'No, never.'

'It is very unfair of him to imply that you should have done something. He can't blame you. It is very selfish.'

'Yes, of course, he was always selfish. Please ring up the police, Robert. It will carry more weight if it comes from you.'

'We are expected at the American Embassy.'

'I can't go. Please apologize for me. Please ring up the police first, Robert.'

She wept most of the night. She blamed herself. She had always known she was a coward.

The next day there was still no news; but the following morning Robert came into her room early with a newspaper which he threw down on her bed.

'There,' he said. 'Look at that.'

There was a photograph of Raymond taken in his younger days. Alison shrank from the word 'death' in the headline, and could not for some moments take in the fact that it was not there.

'Asylum,' she read. 'Moscow? Robert, what is this? I don't understand.'

'He's defected.'

'Defected? But what from?'

She was sitting up in bed with tears running down her cheeks. She had pushed back her uncombed hair as she tried to read the paper and some of it stuck out in a tangle on one side of her head. She looked quite distracted.

'From our side,' said Robert patiently.

She ran her hands through her hair again and now it stood out on either side of her face as if under its own impulse.

'But what is our side?' she cried.

'Do calm yourself. Read it. He's gone to Russia. He went on some tour or other and when they were leaving he said he'd stay. The papers are trying to make out he's a spy.'

'But of course not . . .'

'There's an interview with the German professor who lived next to him. He says he wasn't a Communist but often said he wanted to live in Russia.'

'Of course. He often said that. I think I shall go to Russia, he said. It was just to be annoying.'

'Do stop crying, Alison. He can't possibly have gone to Russia just to be annoying.'

'He wanted to go to faraway parts of Russia, remote and terribly boring. He thought he'd find people who were untouched by the horrible twentieth century and he'd be a doctor and be anonymous and at one with the human condition.'

'Alison, you really must stop crying. You don't usually cry. Don't you see this really is the last straw. I mean it's terribly inconsiderate for one thing. Obviously people are going to think there's more in it than meets the eye. It's going to be quite awkward for me for one thing. I mean people know perfectly well he was a friend of ours. Alison, stop crying. This thing Raymond has done, it's the final frivolity. Can't you see that? The ultimate frivolity.'

Alison nodded vigorously. 'It is. I do see that. It is the ultimate frivolity.'

Seeing that she was by now laughing as well as crying

Robert said shortly, 'You're hysterical. I'd better leave you to pull yourself together.'

★

At that evening's Embassy dinner party the Ambassadress was generally agreed to be in a particularly charming and animated mood. She and the Ambassador, always a good if slightly fussy host, made a distinguished pair. Early in the evening he was seen to seek her out and ask her how she was, and when she answered that she was very well he raised his glass and said with a smile, 'To the Flying Dutchman!' After a moment's pause she smiled in response and, raising her glass, repeated his words. The little scene was thought by those who observed it to be, though mystifying, rather charming.

Certainly it pleased Alison. It was Robert being generous and also acute; at his best. All evening she felt extraordinarily happy. Raymond was in existence. Something of immense value which she had thought she had lost had been returned to her. One day, not now but later – when the children were older, when Robert had a young mistress who was kind as well as pretty – she would go upstairs and fetch the fur coat which Robert had given her, and pack one small suitcase and go to the station. She would travel by train across Europe, crossing frontiers, changing trains at distant stations, arrive late at night, wrapped in her furs, the only passenger, and say in whatever language the people could understand, 'Take me to the house of the English doctor.' She would be taken along an unfamiliar village street and would knock at the door of an unknown house. He would be there. She would go in. He would take off her coat. There would be a stove, and a samovar of tea. They would sit down, and take each other's hands, and look into each other's faces, without fear.